D0227401

Storm Warning

Also From Larissa Ione

~ DEMONICA/LORDS OF DELIVERANCE SERIES ~
Pleasure Unbound (Book 1)
Desire Unchained (Book 2)
Passion Unleashed (Book 3)
Ecstasy Unveiled (Book 4)
Eternity Embraced ebook (Book 4.5) (NOVELLA)
Sin Undone August (Book 5)
Eternal Rider (Book 6)
Supernatural Anthology (Book 6.5) (NOVELLA)
Immortal Rider (Book 7)
Lethal Rider (Book 8)
Rogue Rider (Book 9)
REAVER (Book 10)
AZAGOTH (Book 10.5)
REVENANT (Book 11)
HADES (Book 11.5)
Base Instincts (Book 11.6)

~ MOONBOUND CLAN VAMPIRES SERIES ~
Bound By Night (book 1)
Chained By Night (book 2)
Blood Red Kiss Anthology (book 2.5)

Storm Warning
By Larissa Ione

Rising Storm
Season 2
Episode 2

Story created by Julie Kenner and Dee Davis

EVIL EYE
CONCEPTS

Storm Warning, Episode 2
Rising Storm, Season 2
Copyright 2016 Julie Kenner and Dee Davis Oberwetter
ISBN: 978-1-942299-93-6

Published by Evil Eye Concepts, Incorporated

All rights reserved. No part of this book may be reproduced, scanned, or distributed in any printed or electronic form without permission. Please do not participate in or encourage piracy of copyrighted materials in violation of the author's rights.

This is a work of fiction. Names, places, characters, and incidents are the product of the author's imagination and are fictitious. Any resemblance to actual persons, living or dead, events or establishments is solely coincidental.

Foreword

Dear reader –

We have wanted to do a project together for over a decade, but nothing really jelled until we started to toy with a kernel of an idea that sprouted way back in 2012 … and ultimately grew into Rising Storm.

We are both excited about and proud of this project— not only of the story itself, but also the incredible authors who have helped bring the world and characters we created to life.

We hope you enjoy visiting Storm, Texas. Settle in and stay a while!

Happy reading!

Julie Kenner & Dee Davis

Sign up for the Rising Storm/1001 Dark Nights Newsletter and be entered to win an exclusive lightning bolt necklace specially designed for Rising Storm by Janet Cadsawan of Cadsawan.com.

Go to www.RisingStormBooks.com to subscribe.

As a bonus, all subscribers will receive a free
Rising Storm story
Storm Season: Ginny & Jacob – the Prequel
by Dee Davis

Chapter One

As Ian Briggs drove through the heart of Storm, Texas, he wondered how such a quaint, quiet town had gotten its name.

He also wondered how he could get so lost in such a small town.

Keeping one hand on the wheel of his obnoxiously candy-apple red rental car, he tapped the screen of the non-functional GPS and cursed. Still frozen. The thing had been working fine when he'd picked up the mid-size Ford at the Austin airport, but it had gone on the fritz right after he checked into the bed and breakfast he'd probably never be able to find again. Now he was driving aimlessly around town, hoping to find Houston Street, and wishing he'd put the charger for his phone in his carry-on. It was nestled deep in his still-packed luggage, and he hadn't realized how low he was on juice until he'd already left the B&B to search out Marcus.

As he passed by Cuppa Joe for what must have been the fifteenth time, he gave up being stubbornly male and pulled over to ask directions. He stepped out of the air-conditioned interior and nearly choked on the heat and humidity. In

Montana, it was already cold. But here...God, how did people stand it? It felt wrong to be wearing jeans and a T-shirt when he'd gotten on a plane this morning wearing a parka.

A refreshing blast of cool air and the rich aroma of coffee hit him as he entered the quaint shop. A few people seated at the handful of tables eyed him with varying levels of curiosity or suspicion as he moved to the counter. He nodded in greeting, but it was the curvy woman standing behind it with the shiny black ponytail who drew his interest.

She poured coffee into a big, lime-green mug and slid it to a guy wearing a Double J Ranch baseball cap at the other end of the counter.

"Thanks, darlin'." Double J guy took his coffee to a table, and she turned to Ian.

"Hi," she said, her smile reaching all the way to eyes the color of smooth, dark chocolate. "Can I help you?" She gestured to a blackboard with the daily specials. "The salted caramel latte is to die for."

Her *voice* was to die for. Light and cheery, with a musical lilt and a cute Texas accent. "Actually," he said, "I was hoping you could point the way to Houston Street."

Cocking her head, she narrowed her eyes at him. "You from the media?"

"Montana."

She grinned, and he swore the entire cafe got a little brighter. "In that case, I'll draw you a map."

She turned around to put down the coffee pot, giving him a brief but tantalizing view of her denim-hugged backside. The apron tied at the small of her back in a neat little bow emphasized her hourglass figure, which he admired as she dug into the apron pocket for a pen and notepad and pivoted back around to him.

"Now, this little square is Cuppa Joe..." She gave him directions as she drew little lines, but he didn't hear most of it because he was too distracted by her voice and the way her lips moved as she talked. "...And Houston Street is right there." She marked an X on the napkin with a flourish of her slender hand.

And look at that, she wasn't wearing a wedding ring.

Idiot. You're not here for a fling.

No shit. He wasn't interested in a fling even back at home. He'd never been one to engage in flash-in-the-pan pleasures. He'd always preferred to invest in the long haul, whether he was talking about business, hobbies, or relationships.

But that didn't mean he was blind or dead from the waist down, and the woman whose name tag said "Marisol" was striking.

"I appreciate it." He took the paper from her, and some fool part of him was a little disappointed that she hadn't written her phone number on it.

"Happy to help." She brushed what looked like flour off her apron. "Can I ask what brings you to our lovely little town?"

The explanation would be long and complicated, and he doubted she really cared, so he said simply, "Family."

"Well, enjoy your stay in Storm. Have you been here before?"

"No, but I'm looking forward to seeing more of it." He waved as he opened the door. "And thanks again."

She returned the wave, and for the briefest moment, he thought about going back to order a cup of coffee.

I repeat, you're not here for a fling.

With a mental kick in the ass, he got into his rental, gave the scribbled map a glance, and headed for Houston Street.

It didn't take long to find the Alvarez house once he was on the right street, and he parked alongside the curb in front of the small, run-down home. New boards, differently colored than the rest, marked where someone had made some repairs to the front porch, and the screen door had shiny new hinges.

He smiled as he knocked on the door. Marcus had told him that he'd been making small repairs around the house, exactly as he'd done around the ranch in Montana.

A blonde forty-something woman with stunning green eyes and Marcus's high cheekbones opened the door with a smile. "Hi. Can I help you?"

"Yes, ma'am. Is Marcus here?"

"He's out at the moment." She looked him up and down. "May I ask who's calling?"

He held out his hand. "I'm Ian. Ian Briggs. You must be Joanne."

"Oh." Her brows flew up in astonishment. "Mr. Briggs. Marcus has spoken so much about you. Did he know you were coming?"

"Nah. I wanted to surprise him." Plus, it was a bit of a last-minute decision.

"Well, come inside. He should be home at any moment. He'll be so excited to see you." She stepped aside so he could enter. "Can I get you anything? I just brewed a pot of coffee."

His mind instantly flashed to the beautiful lady at the bakery and his face heated. "Coffee would be perfect."

He took a seat at the kitchen table while she brought him a steaming cup of joe. "I'm so glad you're here," she said. "I want to thank you for everything you did for Marcus."

"It was my pleasure. He's an amazing kid."

There was nothing more beautiful than a mother's pride in her child, and Joanne's smile was radiant. "You have more than a little to do with that, I think."

As much as he'd like to take credit for how Marcus turned out, it wasn't fair. "He told me a lot about you, and if even half of what he said was true, you gave him a great foundation and a lot of love."

She flushed and looked down at the table. "There are a lot of things I'd have done differently." The quiet regret in her voice punched him right in the heart, because he felt the same way about his own past.

About his own son.

Female laughter floated into the kitchen, and a moment later, a dark-haired teen in baggy sweats rounded the corner, followed by a blonde in tight shorts and a skimpy tank top. He recognized both from the pictures Marcus would show him whenever they sent them to his phone.

"Girls," Joanne said, "I want you to meet Marcus's friend from Montana. Ian, these are my daughters, Mallory and Dakota."

"Nice to meet you." Mallory gave him a cheery smile as she snagged a Coke from the fridge. "Marcus talks about you all the time."

Dakota wasn't nearly as friendly, and she gave him the stink-eye as she took a donut from a box on the counter. "Why are you here?"

There were several reasons, but those were between him and Marcus. "I miss your brother, and I wanted to check up on him."

"Why?" The challenge and suspicion in her voice and her gaze reminded him of Marcus, back when Ian first met him. "You aren't Marcus's dad, you know."

There were so many things Ian could say about that, but none of them would have been appropriate to voice to people he'd only known for five minutes.

"No," he said softly. "I'm nothing like Marcus's dad."

"Mom?" Marcus's deep voice boomed through the house, punctuated by the sound of the front door slamming closed. "Whose car is that—" He broke off as he entered the kitchen. "Ian?"

Ian barely had a chance to stand up before Marcus engulfed him in a huge hug. The boy felt good. Solid. Like he'd put on even more muscle.

"It's good to see you, son."

Marcus pulled back, the biggest grin Ian had ever seen on his face. "Why didn't you tell me you were coming?"

He shrugged. "It was spur of the moment. And I figured if I wanted to visit, I'd better do it before the snow sets in."

Still grinning, Marcus raked his hand through his hair, which did nothing to tame the unruly black mop. "Where are you staying?"

"I got a room at the Flower Hill bed and breakfast," he said. "Is that the one where you used to work?"

Marcus nodded. "Mallory works there now. Anna Mae and Rita Mae will take good care of you. Their breakfasts are amazing."

"Totally. Anna Mae makes a mean sausage casserole," Mallory chimed in, "and I don't even like sausage."

Joanne picked up her purse and car keys from off the dining table. "Well, I have to meet with Tate, and I'm sure you two have a lot to talk about, so I'll get out of your hair."

Mallory jerked her thumb toward the hallway. "And I have homework."

"And I just don't care enough to stay." Dakota shrugged. "Ciao."

Everyone took off, leaving Ian with Marcus. "Well," Marcus sighed. "That's my family."

They seemed like a normal, happy family, so much so that Ian never would have guessed that until just a few months ago, they'd been under the thumb of an abusive bastard. As much as he missed Marcus, he was glad Marcus had been able to help his family heal.

"They must be thrilled that you're back," Ian said.

Marcus laughed. "The jury is still out on that." Marcus gave him another hug, and Ian's eyes stung with emotion. It had been a long time since anyone had been this happy to see him. "I'm glad you're here, Ian."

"So am I, son," he said roughly. "So am I."

* * * *

Five minutes after first seeing Ian in the kitchen, Marcus was still reeling. They'd moved out to the back patio, taking seats at the beat-to-hell plastic table.

Marcus took a gulp of his iced tea and shook his head. "I can't believe you came all the way here just to check on me."

"I was worried." Ian smoothed a finger along the curve of his coffee cup's handle as he spoke. He did that with every coffee mug. It was a quirk that had always amused Marcus. "I know you're doing good, but I also know you're worried about your mom and Dakota."

He blew out a long breath. "My mom is in a good place, I think. She's not working for Marylee anymore, so that helps."

Marcus had also caught her flirting with Dillon Murphy while they were both getting gas the other day, and she'd been all smiles since. He'd never seen her so lighthearted, in fact. He just hoped Dillon would tell her the truth about his role in Hector's disappearance. He also hoped Hector would file divorce papers from whatever shithole he was living in, but that was probably a pipe dream. Hector was too possessive, egotistical, and jealous. He wouldn't give up anything he considered his property without a fight.

"But Dakota...I don't know. She's been moody." Marcus reconsidered that. "Well, moodier than normal, with more extreme swings. Sometimes she's sullen and grumpy, and other times she's bouncy and optimistic."

"Bouncy and optimistic are good," Ian offered.

"Not when it's coming from Dakota. It's creepy and wrong. It's like she's waiting for something. Like the mother ship."

Ian chuckled into his glass. "And what about you? You said you got a job on a ranch? They treating you well?"

He nodded, because for the most part, everything was

cool. He'd been afraid Marylee Rush would use her influence to keep him off the ranch, but in the end, he'd gotten the job. And the Johnsons, while not overly friendly, were fair. But some of the ranch hands were certified USDA Prime assholes. Nothing he couldn't handle, but he figured it wouldn't be long before he decked one particular dickhead who kept taunting him about his "lying slut of a sister."

"I can show it to you, if you want to check out the operation," Marcus said, knowing Ian would jump at the chance to tour another ranch. He was always eager to learn new and better ways of running a cattle business. "They do a few things different here in Texas."

As predicted, Ian agreed, and they settled into comfortable conversation. Ian brought Marcus up to speed on life back in Montana, and Marcus unloaded crap he hadn't been able to talk to either Logan or Brittany about.

Like how much shit he took from Brit's father and grandmother. He felt like he always had a target on his back. How were they supposed to have a relationship when he wasn't comfortable—or welcome—at her house, and she wasn't comfortable here with Dakota?

He needed to get a place of his own, but spending the extra money on rent would make it harder for him to help out his mother financially. Plus, as Mallory had pointed out just a couple of days ago, he was probably the sole reason Dakota treated their mother with any respect at all. If he left, Mallory was sure that the house would be ground zero for the next frontier war.

And she was probably right.

The doorbell rang, and he excused himself to see who was at the door. Brittany's BMW was in the driveway, and his heart beat a little faster as he opened the door.

"Hi." She was dressed in his favorite ripped jeans her dad hated and a skimpy lace top he hated even more. Everything she did lately seemed to be tailored to annoy

Sebastian. Funny.

"Hey." He dipped his head to kiss her, lingering just long enough for his neighbors to think it was inappropriate. She tasted like cinnamon sugar and smelled like some wildflower he couldn't place, but it made him want to roll around in a meadow with her.

Reluctantly, he lifted his head and stepped back. "There's someone I want you to meet." Taking her by the hand, he led her to the back patio, where Ian came to his feet. "Ian, this is Brittany. Brittany, Ian."

"So this is the young woman I've been hearing so much about." Ian held out his hand, and Brittany shook it. "It's nice to finally meet you."

"It's great to meet you." She cast a teasing glance at Marcus. "I hope whatever Marcus told you about me was good."

"Every word," Ian said. "Now I see why."

Pink smudged her cheeks and she smiled shyly. Marcus loved how easily she blushed and got flustered. "I didn't know you were coming for a visit. How long are you staying?"

"I'm not sure yet. I haven't taken a vacation from the ranch in years, so I figure I'm due."

"Absolutely," she said. "I hope you can make it an extended stay." She turned to Marcus. "I've only got an hour before I have to be at the computer for a live lecture. I dropped by to see if you wanted to grab a burger or something, but we can do it another time."

"Don't worry about it," Ian said. "You two go get dinner. I need to get back to the B&B and make some calls. I left Rudy in charge."

Marcus laughed. Rudy was a good guy, a solid worker, but sometimes Marcus thought that the cows had more common sense than he did. "Tell him hi for me."

"I will."

Marcus jerked his head toward the back gate. "I'll walk you to your car."

"I'll catch up," Brittany said, giving his hand a squeeze. "I need to use the bathroom and then I'll be right there."

He gave her a quick peck and walked with Ian out to his rental. But before Ian got in, he turned to Marcus.

"I get it now," Ian said.

"Get what?"

"Why you're staying." Ian gestured toward the house. "You've got a good thing here, kid. A real family, nice town, great girlfriend. All of it is worth standing your ground for. I'm proud of you."

Hector had never, not once, told Marcus he was proud of him. And for some reason, a wave of guilt washed over him. When he'd first come back to Storm, he'd been sure he wouldn't be here long. And then he'd decided to stay, but not forever. The plan had always been to go back to Montana and help Ian run the ranch. So why did he feel like he was betraying him?

"I'm going back to Montana," Marcus swore. "I need to be here for now, but I won't let you down."

Ian shook his head and gave him a brief hug. "As long as you're doing what's best for *you*, you won't let me down. See you tomorrow."

Marcus stood there and watched Ian leave. As the car disappeared around a corner, Brittany's arms came around his waist from behind.

"What are you doing?" she asked, her warm breath fanning over his back.

He settled his hand over hers and stroked her smooth skin with his thumb. "Thinking about how lucky I am that it was Ian's ranch I stopped at when I ran out of gas."

"I don't think you're giving yourself enough credit."

He snorted. "If anything, I'm not giving him enough. I was such an asshole back then."

"Back *then?*" she teased, and he laughed.

Times like this, when everyone he loved was nearby and he was as happy as he'd ever been, he could almost believe that everything would turn out.

And maybe, just maybe, it would.

Chapter Two

Marisol Moreno hummed to herself as she mounted the porch steps of the Flower Hill bed and breakfast to deliver their recent order of baked goods, some of them still warm from the oven. She'd been up since four a.m. and, fueled by coffee, had baked for two hours until Cuppa Joe's morning shift arrived to open.

She usually didn't make the deliveries, but she'd been antsy lately, and the bakery's four walls were closing in. She hadn't been able to pinpoint the cause of her acute case of hyperactivity and scattered thoughts, but it was driving her crazy. Luis was doing great in school, the business was thriving, and things were going as well as could be expected with Ginny and her pregnancy, especially now that the media had backed off in favor of other scandals.

Well, whatever it was, she couldn't deny that it was making her remarkably industrious.

She let herself into the B&B through the unlocked front door and went straight to the kitchen, where Rita Mae was mixing what looked like blueberry pancake batter.

"Good morning, Marisol." Rita Mae grinned at her from over her shoulder. "Did you get my message about doubling the order of white chocolate macadamia nut cookies?"

"I did." She lifted the extra-large bag. "You must be expecting a lot of guests."

"The extra cookies are for me," Anna Mae called out as she entered the kitchen from the back, her arms loaded with a big bag of flour and a giant mixing bowl.

"Someone is feeling a little stressed," Rita Mae explained, giving her sister a pointed look.

Marisol loved these two ladies, and she hoped to have the same easy relationship with her own sister when they were older. Right now though, Marisol was too busy playing mom to her siblings.

"Anything I can help with?" she asked.

Anna Mae clucked at her sister but spoke to Marisol. "It's nothing, and my sister has a big mouth."

Rita Mae sniffed haughtily and poured batter onto a hot skillet. Blueberry-scented steam rose up as the batter sizzled. "Better a big mouth than a blind eye."

There was definitely some subtext wafting in the air with the berry aroma, and as curious as Marisol was to know more, she'd always been more of a peacemaker than an instigator, so she changed the subject.

"So...how many guests do you have this morning?" she asked brightly.

"Just Mr. Briggs." Rita Mae gestured with her spatula to the backyard.

Curious, Marisol set the bag of treats on the counter and peeked through the French doors. And oh...oh, my.

It was the tall, dark-haired man who'd asked directions in her bakery yesterday. And he was practically naked, his thickly-muscled body a work of art as he performed a series of martial arts forms. She figured he must be in his late thirties or early forties, but he had the physique of a twenty-two year old, the kind of body that came from long days of hard work, not hours of weightlifting.

"Wow," she breathed, and behind her, Anna Mae

chuckled.

"You should have seen him when he got in from his jog."

"Glistening skin and muscles everywhere," Rita Mae said, appreciation dripping from her voice.

Marisol's mouth went as dry as a store-bought cookie as he lowered his lean body to the ground and started doing pushups. "What did you say his name was?"

"Ian Briggs." Rita Mae flipped the pancakes. "I guess Marcus used to work for him in Montana." She glanced over her shoulder at Marisol. "How's everything at home? Is Ginny doing okay? Is the press still harassing her?"

"Not really. They've moved on to a new scandal. Something to do with that grocer who is running against Sebastian Rush for state senate." Reporters still called the house, and every once in a while a photographer would snap a picture of Ginny in public, but for the most part, the scandal had died down. But only because there was no proof that the baby Ginny carried belonged to a married senator. Once the baby was born, Marisol feared that the paternity test would confirm the worst, that the child would belong to Senator Rush and not Ginny's late best friend, Jacob Salt. "Ginny's doing good. She's taking some online classes and getting ready for the baby."

"She looks adorable in her maternity clothes," Anna Mae said, and was there a note of wistfulness in her voice? She didn't have any children, and at her age, chances were that she never would. Had she wanted them?

Marisol sighed. "She doesn't think so. She held off wearing them as long as she could, but she finally caved in last week." She glanced out the door and nearly broke out in a hot sweat. Mr. Briggs was doing crunches now, and the sight of all those muscles bunching and flexing with each roll of his spine...oh, Lord.

All that antsy she'd been feeling was now in her pants as

her body sputtered to life like a tractor starting up again after a long winter.

Marisol watched, spellbound, as he collapsed onto his back and panted up at the sky. She imagined him lying like that in bed, with a woman straddling his waist while they both recovered from a sexual marathon, and a sweet, pinching ache began to throb between her legs.

He rolled onto his side and his dark, piercing gaze locked with hers through the glass in the French doors. She suddenly felt very, very exposed, as if he was looking right into her brain and seeing the naughtiness that had been playing like a dirty movie in her head.

Heat seared her cheeks and her pulse jumped wildly and holy cow, it was time to get out of there.

"I, ah...I have to go." She wheeled around, banged into the counter, and barely avoided stumbling. *Smooth, Marisol.* Mortified, she gave the sisters a wave and rushed toward the door. "I'll send your weekly invoice later."

Her heart was pounding and she was hot all over, and what was wrong with her? It wasn't as if she'd never seen a man work out before. And it certainly wasn't as if she'd never been turned on. Before her parents died and she'd given up college to raise her siblings, she'd been hella wild.

She winced at the realization that the word *hella* was a part of her vocabulary, thanks to Luis. Then she winced again at the idea that she'd been some sort of rebel. She hadn't been wild, let alone *hella* wild. But she'd had boyfriends and she'd done some experimenting. Becoming the legal guardian to two kids overnight had made her grow up and get serious real fast, though, and she hadn't made time for a man for years.

Not until Patrick.

Patrick.

Shame slammed into her like a punch to the gut. She liked him. A lot. He was sexy and noble and sweet. He wanted her and had made every attempt to take their relationship to the next level. Heck, he'd be happy to just take it public. He'd been so good to her, giving her space and time even though she was sure he didn't understand why she'd been so insistent upon keeping things casual. His patience was yet another quality that made him an amazing man.

But he'd never made her insides quiver or her heart race or her pulse pound at the juncture of her thighs.

God, she was a jerk. She'd told Patrick she needed time because she was too busy with life to actually *have* a life.

But what if the reason she hadn't committed to Patrick wasn't because of how busy she was? What if it was because she hadn't found someone who made her *want* to make room in her life for him?

Not that the someone was Ian Briggs. Obviously. He was only visiting, and it wasn't as if they'd even talked beyond polite chat in the bakery.

So...no, Ian Briggs did not get to make her feel guilty for keeping Patrick at arm's length.

But she couldn't help but wonder if Patrick would ever make her feel like throwing caution to the wind and doing something for herself.

As she started down the steps, she tried to convince herself that her instant attraction to Ian Briggs was nothing.

Absolutely nothing.

* * * *

"Well, that was odd," Anna Mae said as the thud of the front door closing reverberated through the kitchen. "She ran out of here like her pants were on fire."

Rita Mae waggled her brows and canted her head toward the backyard. "Maybe they were."

"Rita Mae!" Anna Mae made an attempt to sound scandalized, but her sister just laughed.

"You act like your innards have never been stirred by a hot man."

"Of course they have." Anna Mae shuffled around the kitchen, gathering the ingredients she needed to make a big batch of hamburger buns for the annual Johnson barbecue this weekend. "But it's been forever."

She regretted the words before they even faded from the air, and sure enough, her sister jumped right on them.

"Not since Chase Johnson," she murmured as she stacked pancakes on a warming plate.

"I don't want to talk about it." And where were the measuring cups?

"You can't ignore it anymore." Ever able to read her mind, Rita Mae gestured to where the cups were sitting next to the flour. "He's back in town."

Anna Mae snorted. "But for how long? He's always been a rolling stone."

"I see what you did there," Rita Mae said in an annoying, singsongy voice. "Chase was a big fan of the Temptations, and he played that song until his guitar strings wore out."

"Didn't I just say I don't want to talk about it?"

"Don't do this, Anna Mae." Rita Mae rounded on her, waving her spatula around like a lunatic to emphasize her words. "Don't keep it all bottled up like you always do. We all know what happens when you finally blow your lid." She jabbed the spatula at her. "You get mean and say things you can't take back."

Well, wasn't that a slap to the gizzard, as their mother used to say. She didn't know what it meant, exactly, but it seemed appropriate in this situation.

"Why don't you say what you're really thinking?" Anna Mae snatched up the mixing bowl. "You think one of those mean things is what chased him away."

One salt and pepper eyebrow went up. Rita Mae really needed to pluck those things. "Was it?"

Anna Mae turned away and slammed the mixing bowl on the counter.

Her sister sighed. "Anna Mae? You've never told me why he left. Not all of it, anyway."

"I told you he wanted to roam the country like a gypsy, playing his guitar for his dinner, and that wasn't the kind of life I wanted."

Strained silence fell in the kitchen, broken only by the hiss of the griddle as Rita Mae loaded it with bacon. Anna Mae knew her sister was dying to remind her that she might have been able to get him to stay if she'd just been honest with him. But it was too late for that. Her secret would stay that way as long as she kept her distance from Chase Johnson.

Because her sister was right. Anna Mae had a bad habit of holding things in and then snapping like a frozen tree branch in a blizzard. She couldn't seem to control her mouth, and when that happened, everything came out. Every thought, every grudge, every curse word she knew she shouldn't say. It was ugly, and she'd spent a lot of time making amends.

But Chase didn't deserve amends. She might have said a few things in anger when he'd told her he was leaving town even if she didn't go with him, but it was ultimately *he* who'd abandoned *her*.

The back door opened and Mr. Briggs came inside, a towel draping his broad, bare shoulders. He inhaled deeply and smiled. "It smells amazing in here."

"Breakfast will be ready in ten minutes," Rita Mae said, "but if you're hungry now, we have muffins, yogurt, fruit—"

He held up his hand with a laugh. "Thank you, but I'm fine. Ten minutes gives me just enough time to shower and dress."

"How was your workout?" Anna Mae asked, grateful for his arrival and the release of the tension in the room.

"It was much needed after a long day in planes and on the road yesterday," he said as he wiped his forehead with the towel. "I saw you had a visitor. The lady who works at the Cuppa Joe."

"Yes, that was Marisol." Anna Mae took a package of sausage out of the fridge and tossed it on the counter next to Rita Mae. "Her little brother is good friends with Marcus's sister Mallory."

"She seemed nice." He moved toward the staircase to the upstairs bedrooms, but at the base, he paused. "Is she...single?"

The way his cheeks flushed pink was adorable on such a rugged man.

"Marisol would have to answer that," Rita Mae said crisply, her voice carrying just a tinge of disapproval.

But did she disapprove of Marisol's are-they-or-aren't-they relationship with Patrick, or did she disapprove of Mr. Briggs's interest?

"It's complicated," Anna Mae said with an apologetic smile. "You know how it is."

He nodded. "Do I ever. See you in a few minutes."

Anna Mae waited until the boards creaked under Mr. Briggs's room to cluck at her sister. "What was that all about?"

Rita Mae shrugged. "I just don't want Marisol to get involved with someone who's going to leave. You of all people should understand that."

She understood that all too well. But she didn't appreciate being reminded. "That's different. Mr. Briggs is a respectable rancher. He's not a faithless drifter who thinks it's okay to leave everyone he loves behind and drop off the face of the earth."

Having said that, she agreed with Rita Mae. Marisol needed to step things up with Patrick, not go running off after some Montana mountain man. Even if said mountain man was a walking advertisement for why single women should move to Montana.

"You said that out loud, you know." Rita Mae propped one hand on her hip and gave her a stern look. "What's going on, hon? Seriously. I know that Chase being back in town has to be bothering you. Talk to me."

Rita Mae was only trying to help, but she wasn't ready for it. "We need more eggs," she said, grabbing her purse. "I'm going to run to the store. Do you need anything?"

Rita Mae just shook her head, a master at conveying withering disappointment without a word. She was just like their mother had been. Rita Mae had also inherited their mother's habit of poking at bears. She couldn't stand being out of the loop on anything, and she pushed and pushed until she got people to talk.

Of course, Rita Mae would say that Anna Mae had gotten their mother's tendency to be judgmental and stubborn and mouthy.

"Anna Mae?" she called out as Anna Mae opened the front door. "Be careful, okay?"

"I'm just driving to the store," she yelled back.

"That's not what I'm talking about." Rita Mae's voice came from right behind her.

Anna Mae looked over her shoulder. "Then I don't know what—"

"Yes, you do." Rita Mae shook her spoon at her. "You either need to make peace with Chase being here, or you need to talk to him and get all that anger out of your system before it comes out on its own. Then, whatever you decide, you need to stay away from Chase Johnson, because I swear, I will not let him hurt you again."

Anna Mae's heart swelled. Her sister had also inherited their mother's fierce loyalty.

Funny, because loyalty was something Chase Johnson knew nothing about.

Chapter Three

Ian was impressed by the Johnsons' cattle operation. Which pissed him off, because some competitive, petty part of him had wanted to own the bigger ranch with the most acreage and the most cattle and the most employees.

As it turned out, Ian owned more property, but the fertile grassland in this part of Texas could support more animals per acre. The Johnson ranch was also less remote, which allowed Zeke and Tucker to modernize a lot easier and more reasonably, cost-wise, than Ian could.

As he and Marcus finished putting away the horses they'd had out all day, Marcus glanced over at him from his big bay's stall. "If you'll give them a couple scoops of grain, I'll put up the tack and brushes."

"You got it." Ian fed the horses and met Marcus outside, where they started up the trail toward the Johnsons' big ranch-style house. Mature live oak trees cast long, late-afternoon shadows across the yard that must take hours to mow. It was probably better than shoveling and plowing snow, though.

Marcus made an encompassing gesture around the ranch. "So what do you think?"

It was beautiful. Dammit. "I have more horses," he

muttered. "And my dog is smarter."

Marcus snorted. "If it makes you feel any better, the cows here are way dumber. I think it's the heat."

Ian laughed out loud. Marcus was good at reading people, and he'd known exactly what to say. "Thanks for bringing me out here and showing me around. Totally different terrain than what I'm used to. The vegetation and landscape are more like what you see in the foothills of the Rockies than what we have out in the plains and badlands of eastern Montana."

"There are a lot more small specialty farms here than where we are in Montana, too," Marcus said, and Ian wondered if he even knew he'd used the "we" in there. "You know, organic, grass fed...there's even someone doing that massage thing with their cattle."

The anvil top of a thunderstorm had formed beyond a distant ridge, and Ian wondered if the thunderstorms here were as dry as the ones they got in Montana. And wait... "Massage thing?"

"Yeah," Marcus said. "You know, they feed their cows beer and give them massages every day and keep them all calm and peaceful. It's supposed to make the meat more flavorful and healthy, because the cows are never afraid, even before they're slaughtered."

"You mean it's like Kobe beef?"

"Yeah, that. Crazy, but they get a gazillion bucks a pound." He shook his head. "Cow whispering is one thing. Cow massaging? *I* don't even get massages."

"Sounds like you need to be a little nicer to Brittany."

Marcus let out a bitter laugh. "We can't find time alone to talk, let alone—" he broke off, a swath of pink staining his cheeks. "You know."

"Yeah," Ian said wryly. "I know. I might not remember how to do it, but I remember what it is."

Marcus glanced over at Ian. "Now that I think about it,

you never brought a woman out to the ranch. But I know you dated. Didn't you? There was that teacher in Miles City."

"Miles City is three hours away." And it wasn't a city. It could barely be called a town. "Carly was nice, but there was nothing there."

"No spark?"

"Not even a little." He hadn't felt that spark since he and April divorced and she took his only son to California to live with the man who eventually killed him. Ian was pretty sure his ability to spark had been snuffed.

An image of Marisol popped into his head, and he reconsidered that. Something about her had definitely lit a spark in him. Not that he could do anything about it, but it was a sign that he wasn't completely ruined.

You knew as much when you let Marcus into your life.

True enough. He'd been broken for so long after his son died, and a dishonorable discharge and time in jail for killing the son of a bitch who had murdered Tyler hadn't helped. Running the ranch after his parole had kept him alive, but he hadn't been *living*. Then Marcus came along, wounded and lost, and they'd healed each other. He was himself again. Just older and wiser and more laid back. And his left knee was shot.

Zeke Johnson came down off his porch and met them at the driveway where Marcus had parked his Impala. "Did old Sorghum treat you well?"

"That sorrel's got spirit," Ian said. "He's a solid ride."

"I've always liked him." Zeke said as he adjusted his cowboy hat, bringing the brim down to block the angle of the bright sunlight. "I've got better cutters, horses with more endurance, but he's got a gait that makes him a pleasure to ride."

"You've got a beautiful ranch," Ian said. "I'd heard there was a drought down this way, but it doesn't look like it hit you."

"It was rough for a while there, but lately we've been lucky. They're still hurting to the east, though, but it's getting better." Zeke gestured toward the house. "Why don't you two come in and have a drink? It'd be nice to talk to someone from up north. I'm sure you do some things differently. All the snow and cold and all."

"I don't miss that." Marcus leaned his hip against his car. "Trying to find lost calves in freezing temps and four-foot drifts? Not fun."

Zeke shivered. "You never said what brought you down here," he said to Ian. "Was it to see Marcus, or are you thinking about taking some of our Texan stock up north? Add a little flavor to your beef?"

Ian didn't take Zeke's words for anything other than what they were, a good-natured jab at the never-ending debate over whether northern or southern beef was the best.

The answer to that question was northern.

"As much as I'd like to, I can't fit 'em in my rental." He tapped the hood of Marcus's car. "We should get going if we're going to meet your mom and Mallory for dinner." Dakota had declined, saying she didn't want to spend time in public, and although Joanne had tried to convince her, everyone seemed relieved when she refused.

Marcus checked his watch. "Crap, I didn't realize it was that late. We still have to shower and clean up." He looked at Zeke. "We'll take you up on a drink another time."

Ian held his hand out to Zeke. "Thanks for letting Marcus show me around the ranch."

"No problem." He turned to Marcus. "And don't forget the barbecue tomorrow afternoon," he said, giving Marcus a clap on the back. "And you too, Mr. Briggs. We'd love for you to come."

"Ian, please. And I appreciate it."

As they drove back into town, Marcus explained some of the things ranchers did different down here, and it became clear that Marcus was doing well. He enjoyed his job and was happy.

But there was something bothering him. Ian couldn't put his finger on why he knew that, but he did. There was a vibe coming off Marcus, a darkness in his eyes that hadn't been there the last time he'd seen him.

"Son, are you okay?"

Marcus gave him a startled look as he turned onto the street for the Flower Hill bed and breakfast. "I'm fine. Why?"

"I don't know. You just seem a little stressed. Like you're always looking over your shoulder."

Marcus's hands tightened on the steering wheel. "Nah. I'm good." He eased the Impala up to the curb. "We'll meet you at Farm to Table in half an hour."

"Perfect."

He watched Marcus drive off, but he wasn't buying his answer. He was too tense. Too evasive. Ian wouldn't push, though; if he'd learned anything about Marcus, it was that he didn't talk until he was ready, and forcing the issue only made him clam up tighter. But the kid was smart, and he'd come to Ian for help if he needed it.

Thunder cracked in the distance, but the leading edge of the storm was close. He figured he had ten minutes before he found out how much rain a Texas storm would bring. Even as he wondered, a drop of rain smacked him in the face, and before he reached the bed and breakfast's porch, he was drenched.

But hey, at least it wasn't snow.

Chapter Four

Patrick Murphy had always loved the big get-togethers his aunt and uncle threw at their ranch. The annual fall barbecue was Patrick's favorite, because the intense summer heat was gone, so the festivities often went late into the wee hours. Once, he, his father, brothers, cousins Tucker and Tate, and Uncle Zeke had sat around the fire pit drinking and laughing until four a.m.

Sitting in church five hours later had been Patrick's idea of hell. To this day, every time he caught a whiff of tequila he heard an overly loud sermon in his head.

A shudder rippled down his body all the way to the grass he stood on. Marcus and Logan stood with him near the pit where a pig turned slowly on a spit, dripping grease onto the crackling coals below.

"Someone step on your grave?" Marcus popped the cap off his beer and tossed it into the metal barrel next to the pit.

"I was remembering a particularly bad hangover."

Logan drained half the lager in his just-opened bottle. "I plan on having one of those tomorrow."

Patrick and Marcus laughed, but concern for his brother put a damper on his amusement. Logan had never been one to try to drink away his problems, and he especially hated hangovers, but lately he'd been hitting the bottle a little too much for Patrick's liking. Not to the level where he was ready to say anything, but he did keep an eye on it.

A phone vibrated, and they all slapped their pants pockets like they were swatting at mosquitoes. It was Logan who ended up with the offending device.

"Oh...shit..." Logan blinked down at his phone, his lips pressed into a grim line.

"What is it?" Marcus leaned toward Logan, who jumped like he'd been caught with his hand in the cookie jar.

"It's nothing." He tried to shove the phone into his pocket, but in his haste he fumbled it.

Patrick lunged, nearly caught it, but it slipped between his fingers. It skipped across the grass, coming to rest at Marcus's feet. Logan dove for it, but Marcus was too fast.

"Don't look, Marcus." Logan held out his hand. "Seriously, man, don't. Give it to me."

Naturally, Marcus didn't listen. Patrick moved next to him to see what the hell had gotten Logan so rattled. The moment he saw the picture, his gut slid into his boots.

It was a mug shot of Marcus, part of an article titled, "Senator's Daughter Dating a Violent Criminal."

Marcus thumbed the screen, scrolling down to the story that gave a rundown of Marcus's police record, including juvenile arrests and school suspensions. It even suggested that he'd been involved in several domestic violence incidents, but it left out the crucial part where he'd never laid hands on his sisters or mother, and had only been defending himself or others from his bastard of a father.

"It's nothing, Marcus," Logan insisted as Patrick read the sorry excuse for journalism over his shoulder. "It's from a radical, fringe political blog that no one will see."

Marcus looked up from the phone. "You saw." His voice was as flat as his eyes.

"Only because I have an alert set up for Senator Rush. I want to know when he uses me to help his campaign."

Marcus looked back down at the screen, his jaw locked hard as he scrolled through the story. He swallowed over and over as he read, like he wanted to puke.

"Hey, man, you okay?" Patrick gripped Marcus's shoulder, because the guy looked ready to take a header. "You look a little queasy."

"This article.. Jesus, it makes it sound like Brittany is in danger, like I'd hurt her. It makes it sound like her parents are begging her to break up with me for her own safety."

Logan took the phone from Marcus, who didn't even seem to notice. He just stood there like it was all he could do to breathe.

Patrick cursed. "This reeks of Marylee Rush."

"It has to be," Marcus said roughly. "She and Sebastian have been trying to break us up. It was only a matter of time before they stepped up the game." He looked them both straight in the eye. "Do *not* tell Brittany. She doesn't need to see this shit."

"It won't change how she feels about you," Logan said. "You know that, right?"

Marcus shook his head. "Yeah, it will. She'll say she can handle it, and she'll believe it when she says it. But she's going to get tired of the looks of pity she'll get. And the looks of scorn because she won't leave me. And the abusive taunts calling her stupid for staying with me. I saw it happen to my mom, and this is a bunch of fucking bullshit we don't need."

Patrick wanted to tell Marcus he was wrong, but he wasn't. That article was going to haunt Marcus as much as his past did.

"Sorry, man." Logan gestured to the bottle in Marcus's hand. "Want another beer?"

"Better not. Wouldn't want to end up in another *alcohol-fueled brawl*," he said, quoting from the hit piece.

"I gotta admit," Logan said, "I didn't hear about any alcohol-fueled brawl."

Marcus winced. "Montana biker bar."

"What about the *rampage of rage*?" Patrick asked.

This time, Marcus gave a full-on grimace as he rubbed the back of his neck. "Country bar in Miles City. Montana arrest number two."

"How about—"

"Oh, hey." Marcus flung his arm out toward one of the picnic tables. "There's Brittany. I'm going to go *endanger* her with my presence."

He took off, and Logan shook his head. "I'm a little worried about him."

"Worried? Why?" Patrick's jaw dropped. "You don't really think he's dangerous, right?"

"What? No, of course I don't." He tipped the bottle to his lips and took a drink. "It's because the Rushes are never going to accept him being with Brittany, and eventually she's going to have to make a choice."

Patrick hadn't thought of that. He couldn't imagine his family demanding that he stop seeing someone, and he damned sure couldn't imagine them being willing to lose him over it. "You don't think Brit'll choose Marcus?"

"Oh, she'll choose him. I'd lay money on it. But she'll lose her family over it. Just like what happened to Marcus's mom when she married his dad." Logan blew out a long breath. "When we were kids, he told me about his parents' fights, and there were a lot that had to do with her family."

Patrick cursed. Marcus had done everything he could to separate himself from his father, and Patrick had no doubt that if he could get rid of the man, right down to his DNA, he would. So to follow in his father's footsteps like that...the psychology of it would only add to the stressful situation.

"And that's the best-case scenario," Logan said, being all grim. He'd been that way since he'd gotten home from the military, but since the shit with Ginny, it had gotten worse. "What if Brittany *does* choose her family over him? I mean, I don't think she will, but it's a lot like what Marcus's mom did to him and why he skipped town and ended up in Montana."

Ouch. "He makes our woman troubles seem petty," Patrick sighed.

"Speak for yourself."

Yeah, yeah. He hated to be unsupportive, but it had been a couple of months now since Ginny had destroyed their relationship, and Logan needed to get back on his feet.

"You should call that redhead who gave you her number at the bar the other night." Patrick had only seen her for a second, but he'd done a double take. "Who was she, anyway? I know pretty much every female of drinking age in this town, and I've never seen her."

Logan idly kicked at the grass with his cowboy boot as he spoke. "She moved here this summer with the Rushes' new neighbors. Those rich people on the hill. I can't remember their names. Anyway, she's their nanny."

"Well, you need to call her." He gave Logan an encouraging but brotherly poke in the shoulder. "She was really into you."

"That's because she'd had three margaritas and a screaming orgasm." Logan rolled his eyes. "She made me make a damned screaming orgasm."

Patrick would have loved to have seen that. Logan hated making frou-frou drinks. "See? She was sending you subliminal messages."

Logan snorted. "Speaking of screaming orgasms, what's going on with you and Marisol?"

Patrick automatically looked around for her, found her across the yard near the badminton net with Marcus's aunt, Hannah Grossman, Patrick's cousin Tara, and a man he'd never seen before. They were all laughing at something he said, Marisol most of all.

"Nothing," Patrick muttered. "Literally nothing is going on with Marisol. I want more than she seems willing to give."

Although she seemed to be perfectly willing to give that stranger her undivided attention. And that laugh had to be fake. It was too perky. Flirty.

Marisol was a lot of things...beautiful, smart, thoughtful...but she was *not* flirty.

"So are you guys together? Not together? Friends with benefits?" Logan waved his hand in front of Patrick's face, dragging his attention away from Marisol and the comedian. "Hey. You with me?"

"Sorry." He jerked his head toward Marisol. "Who is that guy talking to her?"

Logan craned his neck and nodded. "That's Ian Briggs. He's the dude Marcus worked for in Montana."

"That's him?" Patrick scrutinized him a little more, from his black jeans and shirt to his dark, wavy hair. "I'd heard he was in town. But I thought he'd be different."

"Different?"

"You know, older. And ugly. Fat, maybe."

Logan laughed. "You're just jealous because he's hitting on the woman you may or may not have a relationship with."

"Funny, Logan. You're hilarious." Like Ian Briggs, the stand-up comedian. "Now, if you'll excuse me, I'm going to use the bathroom, and then I'm going to go rescue her."

Logan choked on his beer with a little too much drama and laughter. "From what? A good-looking, rich guy who's built like an underwear model? Sure. Good luck with that."

Patrick flipped his brother the bird as he walked off, but he cringed when he saw his cousin Tara's husband and the pastor of their church, Bryce, shooting him a scathing look. A scathing look that turned to flat-out anger when little Danny, walking next to his father, parroted Patrick and raised his middle finger back at him.

Great. He was never going to hear the end of this. He could hear Bryce's sermon already, and he hadn't had a drop of tequila.

Chapter Five

When Brittany agreed to meet Marcus at the Johnson barbecue, it had only been because neither Ginny nor her father would be there. So when she'd seen Sebastian's sporty little Mercedes parked along the side of the driveway, she'd nearly turned around and left. It was bad enough living with him after everything he'd done; she didn't want to see him during her personal time as well.

People milled around, hands full of food or drinks as country music blared and smoke from the pig roast and a barbecue grill billowed into the clear sky. Balloons tied to the backs of chairs bopped in the breeze, reminding her of how she and Ginny had always volunteered to help set up, and their favorite thing to do was the balloons.

A pang of sadness clenched in her chest. She missed Ginny so much. There was a hole in her life that nothing, not even Marcus, could fill. But every time she started to soften toward her former friend, she pictured her in bed with Brittany's father, and all the anger and betrayal came roaring back.

At least the anger numbed the pain.

She strode across the grassy lawn toward the rows of picnic tables, raising her hand to wave at her aunt Celeste and

Mary Louise Prager. Smiling despite the fact that her father was lurking somewhere, she dropped her arm and nearly bumped into some lady's back. She instinctively opened her mouth to apologize, but snapped it shut when she realized the woman with a phone to her ear was her grandmother.

"I just sent you two new photos," Marylee said, her voice cracking like a whip. "Things are getting critical here. You're needed." With that, she tucked her phone into her purse, and Brittany hurried in the opposite direction.

Marcus jogged toward her, and her heart fluttered. They'd been dating for a few months now, but she felt this way every time she saw him.

"Hey." He slowed, and she hastily took his hand.

"Just keep walking," she said, speaking in a near whisper. "I don't want my grandmother to see us—"

"*Brittany.*" Her grandmother's shrill voice called out, and she groaned as she turned around. Marylee raked her gaze up and down Marcus's body, her mouth pinched in disapproval. "Oh. Hello, Marcus, I didn't realize you were working today."

"He's not working," Brittany ground out.

"Of course." Her hand fluttered up to her pearl necklace, the epitome of overly dramatic pearl-clutching. "I'm so sorry. Sometimes it's hard to tell when one is dressed for tending cattle."

Clearly, the gloves were off and her family wasn't even *pretending* to tolerate Marcus. He squeezed her hand, a silent message to not engage. For some reason, he didn't want her to fight with her family about him, especially in public. So as much as she wanted to go off on her grandmother for the passive-aggressive insult, she let it go.

For now.

"Why are you even here?" she asked. "You think barbecues are dirty, smoky, and crawling with bugs." Even as Brittany said it, Marylee swatted at a mosquito.

"Your father and I stopped by with some staffing and

advisor recommendations for Tate. I was just leaving."

"Good. No one wants you here."

Marylee's eyes turned icy. "Young lady," she snapped. "Your father and I have put up with your insolence for months now because of...the situation. But it's about time you—"

"The *situation?*" Brittany broke in, incredulous. "That's what you're calling it?" She laughed bitterly.

"As I was saying," Marylee said in her imperious, scolding voice that used to make Brittany shake in her shoes, "it's time for you to grow up and start thinking of someone besides yourself for once. I am your grandmother, and I deserve respect."

The I-am-the-family-matriarch-and-you-must-bend-to-my-will thing would have worked on Brittany only a year ago. But so much had changed since then. She'd had her world turned upside down and her eyes opened, and in the new, harsh reality she now lived in, her grandmother was a villain.

"I'm sorry, Grandmother, but I can barely look at you and my father, let alone respect you." She yanked on Marcus's hand and dragged him away from there before she started screaming.

"I need a drink," she growled, but Marcus pulled her in the opposite direction of the beverage table.

"I have a better idea," he said. "This way."

She let him lead her down the path toward the stables, fuming the entire way. She was so angry, in fact, that when they walked around to the rear of the stables, she nearly ran into Kristin Douglas as she slipped out of one of the side doors.

"Brittany!" Kristin's cheeks went beet red as she clutched her chest in flustered surprise. "Hi. I was just...you know, looking at the horses. I'll see you back up at the house." She brushed past them and hurried up the path.

"Was that weird?" Brit glanced between Kristin's

retreating form and Marcus. "That was weird, right?"

"Which part?" He twined his fingers with hers and led her around back.

Figuring his question was rhetorical, she didn't answer. She was too busy trying to not step in horse crap.

"Where are we going?" The earthy smell of horses and dirt and wood filled the air more strongly with every step. "Why didn't we go through the front?"

"Because this entrance will take us inside the hay room." He grinned as they ducked through the door. "I wanted a little privacy."

"Oh—!" She broke off as he spun her against a wall of hay and then pressed his long, lean body against hers. "Oh."

His smile made her swoon—honest to god swoon. The impish glint in his mocha eyes said he knew it. He was so cocky sometimes.

She loved it.

She loved it even more when he dipped his head and kissed her like there weren't fifty people roaming around outside. He tasted like powdered sugar and almonds, which meant Marisol must have brought a batch of cookies to the barbecue, but there was nothing sweet about what he was doing with his tongue.

Suddenly, he broke off the kiss. "Did you hear that?" He cranked his head around, and from over his shoulder she got a glimpse of someone slipping out of the stable.

"Who was that?"

"I don't know," he said. "Ranch hand, maybe. I didn't get a good look."

Realization dawned, and she grinned. "I'll bet that was why Kristin acted so strangely. She was out here with a man."

One dark eyebrow shot up. "You think?"

"I hope." She trailed her finger over the hard planes of his chest, wishing they were somewhere much more private. "She seems lonely."

"I'm lonely too." A naughty grin turned up the corners of his mouth as he swept her into the sectioned-off area at the back of the stables and lifted her onto a stack of baled hay. He remained standing, moving to settle himself between her spread legs. One hand came up to caress her cheek as he leaned in, bringing his mouth to hers...

"Marcus?" Joanne's voice rang out, and they froze. "Are you here?"

Marcus put his finger to Brittany's lips and shook his head. His message was clear; he didn't want to spoil this time alone, not even for his mother.

"Joanne?" The new voice belonged to Dillon Murphy. Ugh. Was the party moving to the freaking stables?

"Dillon." Joanne sounded winded all of a sudden. "What are you doing here?"

Heavy footsteps thudded on the concrete floor. "I followed you."

"You shouldn't have done that."

The footsteps came to a halt. "Well, why are *you* here?"

"I dropped off some paperwork for Tate." There was a tremor in Joanne's voice now. Was she nervous?

Very quietly, Marcus peeled away from Brittany and climbed up on the hay bale stack to peek over the top. She joined him so they were shoulder to shoulder, looking down on where Dillon and Joanne were standing a foot apart, their body language indicating that there was more going on here than just a casual conversation.

"But why are you in the stable?" Dillon asked.

"I'm looking for Marcus." Joanne gave a cursory glance around. "Travis said he saw him here."

Travis? Brittany frowned. She hadn't even seen her uncle yet, let alone here at the stables. Had Travis been the man they'd seen slipping out of the building?

"Why are you looking for Marcus?"

Joanne huffed at Dillon's question. "Is this an

interrogation, Sheriff? Are *you* looking for Marcus? Because he hasn't done anything wrong."

"Whoa." Dillon's head snapped back. "Joanne, what's going on? Where is this coming from?" When she didn't answer, just looked away, Dillon reached out and tilted her face toward him in a gentle, loving gesture that stole Brittany's breath. "Hey. Whatever it is, you can trust me."

"When I'm with you, I can't trust *myself*," she whispered.

Brittany glanced at Marcus for his reaction, but his expression was unreadable. When she looked back to the couple, she let out a surprised gasp at the sight of Joanne and Dillon kissing. It only lasted a few seconds before Joanne shoved away from Dillon, her face etched with misery.

"I'm sorry," she rasped. "I can't do this. I'm married."

Dillon stepped closer, not giving an inch. "Hector's gone, Joanne. You're free."

"No, I'm not." Her voice was pleading. Desperate. It broke Brittany's heart. "There's such a huge focus on our family now. I can't be seen with you, and I refuse to sneak around."

"You can get a divorce," Dillon said, a note of desperation in his voice now. "Even if you can't locate your spouse, you can file. I checked."

Joanne smiled, but it faltered within seconds. "I still need to stay away from you. If Hector were to ever find out we've kissed, if he came back…" She shook her head, and at her side, her hand trembled. "He'd kill you."

"Joanne—"

"Don't." She held up her hand to stop him. "I need to go home. I'll talk to Marcus later."

"Wait. You never said why you're upset."

She hesitated, but a few heartbeats later, she dug into her purse and pulled out her phone.

"It's about Marcus." She handed it to Dillon. "I wanted him to see this news piece before somebody blindsides him."

"Jesus," he murmured. "This is...bad."

"Those damned Rushes," Joanne said, and Brittany's gut twisted. What had her family done now? "I wish I still worked for Marylee so I could scrub the toilet with her toothbrush, fill her shampoo bottle with hair remover cream, and then quit my job when all the phones are ringing."

Dillon cocked a dark eyebrow, but his voice dripped with approval. "You're downright diabolical."

She gave him a sly smile. "How do you think I got back at Hector when he pissed me off?"

Laughing, he handed the phone back to her. "Come on. I'll walk you back up to the house. Marcus will get past this."

Get past what? Marcus's expression still didn't offer any clues except that whatever they were talking about wasn't news to him.

"He shouldn't have to get past anything," Joanne said. "I adore Brittany, but I can't see things ending well for her and my son. Sebastian and Marylee will never let it happen, and I fear the lengths they'll go to. I see how they destroy political opponents, people with power. Our family doesn't stand a chance if they bring everything to bear on Marcus."

"You know I've got your back, Joanne. Yours and Marcus's."

"I know." Joanne smiled at him, but worry darkened the crescents under her eyes.

They walked out, together but far enough apart to not raise suspicion, leaving Brittany confused and shaking. She couldn't even look at Marcus, but she could tell by his silence that he definitely knew what his mother and Dillon had been talking about.

"What was it, Marcus? What did she show Dillon?"

He sighed and tapped on his phone, bringing up a political site. When he handed her the phone, she looked in horror at the article on the screen. The author made Marcus sound like a violent, drug-addicted fiend, and it made her sound like a victim who, despite her parents trying desperately to help, refused to leave her abuser. Never mind that Marcus had never hurt her. Not even close.

Her eyes stung with tears. "My God," she whispered. "They're never going to stop, are they? My father and grandmother are going to keep hitting you over and over."

"I can handle myself, Brit," he assured her. "Don't worry about it. No one cares about that stupid article. Half the town already thinks I'm a worthless criminal, so it's not news."

The idea that anyone could believe Marcus was worthless made the tears start to flow, and she dashed them away with the back of her hand. "I'm just so sorry. You shouldn't have to deal with this because of me."

He reached out and caught a tear with one finger, his touch so tender that it only made more tears fall. "I'll deal with it just fine if it means I get to keep you."

He was so sweet, but deep down, she had her doubts. What his mother had said was true. Her father and grandmother would never give up on trying to destroy her relationship with Marcus, and she worried about how far they'd go. She'd seen them take down their political opponents without mercy. Worse, she'd seen them *enjoy* going in for the kill. It had never really bothered her before...after all, she'd grown up with it, knew the political world, and understood that it was a dirty, dirty business.

But now that her blinders had come off, she could see clearly for the first time in her life. And the truth of the matter was that her family was ruthless, bloodthirsty, and Marcus was in their crosshairs.

Chapter Six

Marisol was having the best time at the barbecue. Things had been so crazy for so long, and this day of doing nothing but enjoying herself felt like a little slice of heaven. She wished Ginny had come, but she understood why her sister had stayed home. There were too many unfriendly faces—*hostiles*, as Luis called them, as if the townspeople were monsters from his video games. Ginny didn't want to deal with the whispers and cold stares, but mostly she wanted to be as stress-free as possible for the baby's sake.

At least Luis had come along once he heard that Mallory and Jeffry would be here but Lacey Salt wouldn't. He was still angry at her for lying about their relationship, and Marisol couldn't blame him. Lacey was a good kid, though, and Luis was generous with his forgiveness, so Marisol figured they'd be friends again soon.

She looked over at where he was playing a spirited game of badminton with Mallory, Jeffry, and Mary Louise, but then Ian, standing next to her, said something funny and she had to laugh.

God, he was...forbidden. Yes, that was the word for him. There were too many obstacles in the way, from the logistics of where they lived, to the limited amount of time she had for a relationship, to the fact that she was sort of dating Patrick.

Patrick, who had been nothing but wonderful and patient with her, and who wouldn't understand if she so much as looked in another man's direction after she'd been so insistent that she didn't have the ability to commit to *anyone*.

She'd actually tried to avoid Ian when she first saw him a couple of hours ago, and aside from a polite smile and a brief hello, she'd been successful in her avoidance. But then, while she was chatting with Hannah and Tara, he'd walked up and introduced himself to them, and that fast, she was trying to talk without sounding like a complete idiot.

"How do you like our little corner of Texas?" Tara asked him after taking a sip of her iced tea. Marisol had tried to talk her into a cup of the homemade sangria she'd brought, but Tara rarely drank. Especially not when Bryce was around.

"Everything in your corner of Texas is beautiful," Ian murmured, and her heart nearly tripped over itself when he gave her a wink. At least, she thought that's what it was. Maybe he had dust in his eye.

"Yes, but you have mountains," Hannah said with a little sigh. "I'd love to see the Rockies."

Tara nodded. "Me, too. I want to try skiing someday."

Ian's gaze locked on Marisol. "What about you?" His voice went low, vibrating her in places that hadn't been vibrated in a long time. "Would you like to see what Montana has to offer?"

Oh, sweet baby Jesus, *yes*. But enough was enough. It was time to draw a line in the sand and stop being charmed by him.

"We have mountains here, you know," she said.

He laughed, genuine amusement crinkling his eyes. "You have what we northerners call 'speed bumps.'"

"Hmph." She tried to sound grumpy, but dammit, that line she'd just drawn had been blurred. "Can we compromise and call them hills?"

His grin...oh, Lord, his grin. "I'm good with that."

Tara shouted something at Bryce about Danny, and then she turned back to the group with a huff. "I warned Bryce that Danny is in a ketchup phase and that he puts it on everything. Including people. Do you think he listened?"

Hannah held up her hand. "I'm going to guess no. Seeing how Tate's shirt is splashed with something red and he's heading toward the house."

Marisol cringed at that. Tate wasn't exactly a kid-friendly kind of guy. He wasn't mean or anything, but he was clearly uncomfortable around them.

"Do you have any kids, Ian?" Tara asked, and the haunted shadows that instantly flickered in his eyes made Marisol uneasy. There was a story there, one she wasn't sure she wanted to hear.

"No biological kids, no," he replied. "What about you, Marisol?"

"Not...technically." She poked at a grape floating in her sangria. "I've spent most of my adult life raising my brother and sister."

"Their parents were killed in a car accident," Hannah explained, thankfully sparing Marisol from having to tell the story. "She's done an amazing job with her brother. And sister, of course," she added quickly. Marisol must have looked hurt, because Hannah reached over and put her hand on her wrist. "You know I didn't mean anything."

"I know," Marisol said. Hannah had never been judgmental, and if anything, she'd been supportive of Ginny's efforts to get her life back on track. Still, the Founders' Day fiasco was so recent that the tarnish of that day clung to Ginny and made everyone uncomfortable when the subject came up.

"Hey, ladies." Patrick joined them, stopping to stand next to Marisol, close enough that their arms touched. He held out his hand to Ian. "Hi, I'm Patrick."

"Ian Briggs." They shook hands, and maybe it was just her, but she swore she sensed an undercurrent of testosterone flowing between them. Could it be that Patrick was jealous?

"So, Mr. Briggs," Patrick said, shifting his stance so he was even closer to her. "I hear you're from Montana. How long do you plan to stay in Storm?"

Ian squared his shoulders and faced Patrick like a bull confronting a rival. "I haven't decided. I thought maybe a couple of days, but I'm finding more and more reasons to stay longer." His gaze dropped to her, for no more than a heartbeat, but she felt Patrick stiffen beside her.

Oh, shit.

Her mind spun, looking for a fun, neutral topic or better yet, an escape route. As luck would have it, she was saved by Brittany. Well, she was saved by the excuse of Brittany.

"Oh, hey, can you all excuse me?" She gestured to where Brit and Marcus were walking toward the house from the direction of the stables and corral. "I need to catch Brittany."

She took off before anyone could protest or offer to come with her, and she caught the young couple near the snack table.

"Hi, guys," she said. "Brittany, can I talk to you for a minute?"

"Go ahead," Marcus said. "I'll go get us some drinks. Marisol, do you want something?" He gestured to her cup. "A refill?"

"Thanks, I'm fine."

He gave Brit a peck on the lips and sauntered away, leaving Marisol alone with Ginny's best friend. She would not say *ex*-best friend.

They hadn't talked much since the disaster on Founders' Day, and she figured a mutual desire to avoid an uncomfortable conversation might have something to do with that. After all, Marisol's sister had slept with Brittany's father, ruining their friendship and Brittany's family.

It was, at least, a good sign that Brittany was smiling. "It's good to see you, Marisol."

"You too. I miss having you around."

Brit's smile wavered. "Well, you know."

"I know." Marisol hesitated, unsure how to bring up what was sure to be a painful topic. "Look, I can't pretend to know how you felt when you found out what happened with your dad and Ginny, but I wanted to see if there's any chance, any chance at all, that you can forgive her someday."

It was only then that she noticed that Brit's eyes were red-rimmed. She'd been crying, and now her eyes went liquid again.

"I don't know," she said. "I really don't."

"She misses you." It had killed Marisol to see her sister in tears the other day as she thumbed through pictures of Brit and Ginny in high school and at slumber parties. "Just this morning she talked about how she wished you two could go to the barbecue together the way you have for years."

"I wish that, too," Brittany said, giving Marisol some much-needed hope.

"Just know that you're welcome at our house any time."

"Thank you." Brittany offered a shaky smile. "I miss you. I've always thought of you as kind of an older sister."

Marisol wrapped her arms around her and squeezed her tight. "Oh, honey, I miss you too." She pulled back and fetched a tissue from her purse. "Here. Your mascara is running."

"Ugh." Brit took the tissue and dabbed at her eyes. "Thank you for the heads-up."

"I got your back." Marisol hesitated, unsure if she should test the boundaries of their newly forged sister-friend status. Ultimately, she decided to take the risk. "Brittany, I know I don't have any right to ask this, but if you could just talk to Ginny—"

"I can't." She reached over and squeezed Marisol's hand. "I'm not ready. I hope you understand."

"Of course." Disappointed but not surprised, Marisol gave Brit another brief hug. "It was good to talk to you."

"You too."

Brittany took off, heading toward the bank of ice chests where Marcus was talking to Ian. As if Ian knew Marisol was looking, he turned, his bold gaze meeting hers.

She waved like a little girl with a schoolyard crush, and feeling utterly foolish, she made a beeline for Mrs. Johnson, who looked like she needed help filling the chip and dip bowls.

And as she opened a bag of corn chips, she wondered whose eyes she felt burning into her back.

Patrick's...or Ian's?

Chapter Seven

"Sorry about the shirt, Tate."

Tate smiled thinly at his sister from where he was standing in the living room with their dad as she walked by on her way to the bathroom.

"It's okay. Ketchup comes out." Under his breath, he added, "Probably." His shirt was in the wash, so he was making do with one of his dad's T-shirts from his last campaign.

Tara paused at the hall entrance. "Joanne wasn't here long, and she left in a hurry. I hope everything's okay."

"Everything's fine," he said, but he felt like a piece of crap for calling her out here on a Saturday. Unfortunately, he was leaving for Austin in the morning to attend a campaign rally for Senator Rush, and he'd wanted to go over some things with Joanne before he left. "We had some last-minute business."

Tara shook her head. "You work too much. Get outside and have some fun." She wagged her finger at him. "No more business today." Having played the mother card she'd perfected since having kids, she disappeared down the hall.

His dad raised his glass of Scotch in salute. "I'm proud of you, son. With your ambition, you're going to do well in the political arena."

It was strange hearing that from his father, who had been so hurt the day he'd said he didn't want to work on the ranch. To Zeke's credit, they still had a good relationship, but he knew his dad had taken it personally.

"I...appreciate that," he said, feeling a little awkward.

"Just watch your back."

"I'm a lawyer, Dad. I've been dealing with backstabbers since law school."

"Not like this." Zeke lowered his voice. "The corruption is corrosive. Power is seductive. It doesn't happen all at once." He rattled the ice in his glass and stared into the backyard, where Luis Moreno and Jeffry Rush were kicking around a soccer ball. "It starts with something small, a favor for a favor. A powerful politician asks you to show your employee an article about her son, and you justify it to yourself by saying you wanted her to see it before it gets around town."

Heat seared Tate's cheeks. Somehow his dad knew that Sebastian had forwarded Tate the link to a nasty article about Marcus and had asked him to pass it along to Joanne. Of course, Sebastian had played it off as being "concerned" about her, but Tate knew that was bullshit. He also knew that by agreeing to do as Sebastian asked, he'd earned himself a favor.

And his dad had just called him on it.

"I'd want to know about that article if it was *my* son," he said, sounding defensive even to his own ears.

"See? You're justifying it." Zeke gave a slow, resigned shake of his head, and an uneasy feeling churned low in Tate's belly. "It's okay. I get it. Politics is dirty business. All I'm asking is that you watch yourself. It's easy to keep moving your ethical line just a few more inches south."

The unsettled sensation solidified in Tate's gut. "You sound like you know something about that."

Zeke cleared his throat and nodded. "I like to think that I've been a good mayor. No, I know I have." He took an extra-healthy swig of his Scotch. "But there are a few things I did that I'm not proud of. They were for the greater good, but that doesn't mean I don't have pangs of conscience about them."

Wow. That was as raw and honest as his father had ever been with him. "Did you ever talk to Mom about it?"

"She's always been my moral compass." Zeke shrugged. "Of course, it would have helped to talk to her before I did these things."

Tate wondered if he'd have been able to confide in Hannah when things got tough. They hadn't really talked about their work, mostly because he didn't think his legal stuff was that interesting to her, and he sure as hell didn't find anything remotely fascinating about her job.

"Hey," Zeke said, gesturing to Danny, who had joined the boys out back. Which meant an adult must be somewhere close by to watch him. "I'm going to take Danny fishing. I know you're not a big fan of outdoor sports, but would you like to go?"

Not a fan? That was a huge understatement. Tate would rather spend the day tangled in a barbed wire fence than on a rickety boat with a hyper kid and a fishing pole.

"Thanks, I'll pass." He frowned. "Bryce is letting you take Danny out on the lake? In a boat? By yourself?"

Zeke chuckled. "I have to take Alice or you or Tucker with me."

He bristled at his brother's name. "It's still a big step for Bryce."

"Huge." Zeke set down his empty glass on the kitchen table. "But I figure he'll change his mind at the last minute or tell Tara to come with us." He gestured toward the front door. "I have to get the burgers going. Do you mind getting more mesquite chips from the garden shed?"

Nodding, he walked outside with Zeke and peeled off to head toward the shed. He was within ten yards when a high-pitched yell pierced the air.

"Help! Help us!"

Heart pounding, he raced toward the voice, running down the path toward the stables. Another voice joined in, and the blood froze in his veins.

Hannah.

"I'm coming!" He looked around, trying to pinpoint the location of the pleas. There. Off the path and over the ridge.

He ran up the hill, expecting the worst, so as he topped the rounded, grassy ridge, he braced himself.

"I'm here," he called out. The other side of the hill was rockier, and down at the base, peering into a gully, was Hannah. Next to her, his little niece, Carol, was waving wildly at him.

"Uncle Tate!" she cried. "Hurry!"

What the hell? He picked his way down the slope, and just before he reached them, Hannah straightened and turned away from the gully.

"Sorry," she said with an apologetic shrug. "You didn't need to run. Carol got a little excited."

Carol pointed into the ravine. "I dropped my doll, and Uncle Tucker went to get it, but now he's stuck."

"What?" He moved over to the edge of the gully, and sure enough, a few feet down, Tucker was looking up at him, his cowboy boot wedged between two rocks. Tate figured it was too much to hope that his brother would be nursing a nice sprain after this.

"I would have gone down there," Hannah said, "but I didn't want to leave Carol up here by herself."

"Here," Tucker called up to them before tossing the doll into the air. "Catch."

Tate caught it one-handed and gave it to his niece.

"Thank you, Uncle Tate," Carol said, hugging the doll to

her chest. "I have to go tell Danny you saved her." She started up the hill, but Hannah grabbed her.

"Hold on, sweetheart."

"Go ahead." Tate gestured up to the house. "I'll get Tucker. I've been saving his ass since we were kids."

She hesitated, and he wondered what was running through her cheating head. Did she think he was going to murder his brother once she was gone or what? Finally, mercifully, she agreed, leaving him alone with his brother.

"You aren't going to help me, are you?" Tucker's voice drifted up from the gully. "You're going to make me have to chew off my own foot."

Tate made him sweat for a few seconds before he looked down at Tucker. "I should leave you there, but there are witnesses," he said, only half-kidding. It would serve Tucker right to rot in the gully for a few hours while everyone else was having fun at the barbecue. Too bad Hannah would miss him. "What will you give me?"

Tucker shielded his eyes from the sun with his hand as he looked up at Tate. "I'm guessing I can't buy your help with a Matchbox car this time, huh?"

"You couldn't buy my help with a real car."

A mild curse drifted up from the gully. "What do you want?"

Tate had always prided himself on his self-control and his ability to watch his mouth. But this time, his answer came before he could think better of it. "I want you to break up with Hannah."

"Screw you." Tucker glared, his eyes flashing with anger. "You had your chance with her. You can't have her back."

"I don't want her back," Tate said, and it surprised him to realize it was true. So was what he said next. "I just don't want you to have her."

"You're an asshole."

Tate thought about how he'd done Sebastian Rush's

bidding by alerting Joanne to the article in order to secure future favors.

"No," he said as he started down into the gully to free his brother, "I'm just a politician."

Chapter Eight

As Chase Johnson looked out at the people enjoying the massive annual barbecue, he couldn't help but believe that if he wasn't staying here with his brother and his sister-in-law, he wouldn't be invited.

Nervous energy made his stomach sour as he finally joined the party. He hadn't felt well this morning, so he'd stayed in his room until this afternoon. And maybe, just maybe, he was stalling a little.

As he walked through the grass, his gaze constantly swept the crowd in case Anna Mae was nearby. Running into her was the last thing he needed right now.

He fielded a lot of, *It's good to see you*s and *How have you been*s and *How long are you staying*s and it was the last that was the most difficult.

He'd been testing the waters for a permanent stay in Storm, and so far, the waters had been shark infested.

His brother didn't want him here, Anna Mae's glares were sharp as blades, and her sister's were only slightly less sharp. He probably deserved it, but neither of them would give him the time to explain. He'd run into Rita Mae last night at the grocery store, and he'd only gotten a few words in before she gave him a warning to keep away from her sister that had included the threat of an iron skillet and the bashing of his skull.

She hadn't changed at all.

Women were crazy.

"Hey, Chase?" Zeke walked past him with an armful of burger buns, and his stomach growled. He hadn't had a burger made with Double J beef and one of the Prager sisters' homemade buns in years. "Would you grab the paper plates and condiments? You know, unless you plan on falling off the face of the earth again anytime soon."

Grinding his molars, Chase started for the house to grab the plates, but screw it. He was tired of his brother's snide comments and disapproving scowls, and he pivoted back around.

"If you don't want me here, why don't you say it? Just go ahead and say it."

Zeke plopped the buns on the picnic table and swung around to Chase. "I can't."

"Why not?"

"Because Alice would kill me."

"And that's the only reason?"

Zeke angrily shoved his hand through his thick head of gray hair. "What do you want me to say? That I'm happy you're back? Why should I be? You never stay. You're here just long enough for people to let down their guards, and then you're out the door again. Last time you skipped out on the rent you owed Mr. Raeburn. I had to pay it, and I lost the deposit money I loaned you when you moved in."

Oh, shit. He'd forgotten about that. Mostly. "I told you I was sorry."

"No, you didn't."

"The card must have gotten lost in the mail." He hadn't sent a card, and going by the skepticism on Zeke's face, his brother suspected as much. "Aren't you even going to ask how long I'm going to stay?"

"Nope." Zeke folded his arms across his chest, going

full-on mule. "Don't care. You're welcome to stay until the end of the month, and if you're still here then, you'd better decide what you're going to do."

Chase felt like he'd been sucker punched. He'd made mistakes...he'd made a lot of mistakes. But he'd always remembered to send presents for the kids at Christmas and for their birthdays, and when they'd gotten older, he'd sent graduation gifts. No matter where he was, he kept an eye on news that came out of Storm, and he'd always gotten a kick out of seeing his mayor brother talk to the media.

"Guess I'll go get the condiments myself." Zeke walked away, leaving Chase alone and feeling like crap.

He wandered around, chatting with everyone who didn't think he was little more than a vagrant, and as he ate his burger and the fall-off-the-bone roast suckling pig, he talked with Tara and her family, reconnecting.

"You know what this party needs?" Tucker asked as he joined their little group at the picnic table. "Some guitar music."

Chase's blood froze. "I don't think so. I just ate, and I drank too much beer..."

"I haven't seen you with a single beer," Tara said, clearly not buying his excuse. "Come on, Uncle Chase. We want to hear you play."

Carol clapped her hands, and her filthy, ragged doll fell to the ground. "Please, Uncle Chase?"

"Please?" Danny joined in, putting down the ketchup bottle he'd been playing with to give Chase big puppy-dog eyes.

As much as he didn't want to do this, he didn't have a good reason to refuse. So, with great reluctance, he fetched his guitar from his room and sat down in one of the chairs near the bonfire Zeke and Tate had built when the sun began to go low on the horizon.

As he took the well-used instrument out of its case, he

ran his fingers lovingly over the smooth wood and rounded curves. She was a lady who had never hurt him, who had been there for all his important moments, the good and the bad, the highs and the lows.

I've neglected you lately. But it's not you, it's me.

Closing his eyes, he plucked at a string. There it was, a sound like a lover's whisper. He did it again and again, letting the tones fill his soul. As his nerves settled, he started playing in earnest. Drawn to the music, everyone gathered around, the energy in the air building like an electrical storm, and pretty soon it turned into a sing-along and a dance contest.

He lost track of how long he played, but he knew when he'd played too long. It was the tremors. The stinging sensation in his fingers. He was in the middle of a song and there was no way he could stop without raising questions. But he kept missing notes and he suddenly felt very, very out of tune.

No one seemed to notice, but damn, he was sweating. His focus was narrowing and shifting, and when he looked up from his guitar, to his horror, the world spun. Or maybe it was the dancing, but either way, he felt as if he was coming apart at the seams.

Somehow he made it to the end of the song, and he put on a big smile and waved. "Thanks, everyone, but I'm done. You were a great crowd tonight."

There was laughter and clapping, and then everyone went back to partying, and he got to try to put away his guitar without shaking like a leaf.

"I didn't think it was possible for you to play worse than you did when you left," Anna Mae said as she strutted past him, nose in the air.

Her words stung even though he knew she was lying. She used to love to listen to him play. But as music and wanderlust took time away from her, she began to resent his guitar. And later, him.

Jogging, he caught up to her before she got to the house. "Annie—"

She snarled at him from over her shoulder. "You do not get to call me that. Not anymore."

He'd always called her that. Hell, he was the only person brave enough to do it. The fact that he no longer had that privilege hit almost as hard as his medical diagnosis had.

"Fine," he said wearily. "But we should talk."

She kept marching, head high, spine so stiff he figured it would snap if he touched her. Not that he would do that. She'd bite his hand off and give him rabies.

"About what?"

God, he hated it when she did that. When she was being difficult for the sake of being difficult. "What the hell do you think?" He picked up his pace, determined to stay next to her. She'd always walked freakishly fast when she was being pissy. Those long legs could *move*. And they could wrap around a man's waist and make him beg for mercy. Of course, his waist had been a lot smaller back then. "We need to talk about the fact that I'm back in town and we're going to run into each other."

"Obviously, we're going to run into each other." She waved her hand dismissively, the rings she'd worn for years glinting in the light from the tiki torches that lit the path to the porch. "I knew you'd be here today. I just assumed you'd have the good grace to stay away from me."

"Dammit, Anna Mae," he sighed, too exhausted to play nice. "I'm not going to live like that. Life's too short." His recent diagnosis had made that very clear to him.

Stopping suddenly, she rounded on him, her expression a strange mix of anger and what he could only describe as fear. But of what? "Does that mean you plan to stay?"

He didn't have a choice. And after a life of total freedom, of sleeping where he wanted, of eating what he wanted, of drinking all he wanted, the lack of choice tasted bitter. Now it was all slow down, eat healthy, exercise, take your medicine, and make good with the family.

"Yes, I'm going to stay."

Her expression fell, and for the first time since he'd been back, he saw the age in her face. Anna Mae had always been a striking woman, and that hadn't changed. But she had a few more wrinkles, a lot more white hair, and her lips weren't as full as he remembered.

Her snort of derision was the same, though. "What does Zeke say about you hanging out like a stray dog? I'm sure he loves having you around." The sarcasm had gotten a little old, too.

"As a matter of fact, he doesn't." The pain of admitting that was sharper than he expected.

"So you're just going to hang out, all unwelcome, at your brother's place?"

Chase waited until after Bryce walked past with Carol before he answered in a lowered voice. "Anna Mae, I know I let you down. I know I left you—"

"Yeah, you left me," she snapped. "You left and never looked back. You never called or wrote. I had to hear about your exploits through the grapevine. Did you even miss me?"

"Of course I did." His heart had ached for her. He'd kept her picture with him at all times, taking it out often, usually while in a drunken stupor, to study her eyes, her lips, the lush body he used to worship with his own. "I missed you every damned day."

She sneered. "I might believe you if you'd ever once called."

He'd tried. Several times. But he always hung up before she answered.

"I couldn't," he said, swallowing the raw note in his voice. "I couldn't bear to hear your voice." He tucked his trembling right hand into his pocket, afraid she'd notice. Afraid she'd see his weakness and pounce on it like a coyote on a wounded rabbit. "If I had, I might have wanted to come back."

"And would that have been so bad?" She watched him expectantly, as if she was hoping for an answer that would ease the pain he'd caused her.

"Yeah. Back then, it would have. I needed to get away, Annie." He'd felt trapped in this small town. His soul had demanded excitement and adventure and freedom, and the mere thought of settling down, even with a woman he loved, had filled him with dread and fed his depression.

"You needed to get away more than you needed to be with me," she said quietly. "You needed to get away *from* me."

She looked so vulnerable, so fragile, and his mind flashed back to the day he'd told her he was leaving—with or without her. Even now, she pressed her hands to her belly the same as she'd done back then, as if she was going to throw up.

"It wasn't you, Anna Mae, I swear." Instinctively, he reached for her, but she sidestepped, and his hand fell to his side. "Please believe me. I needed to get away before I lost my mind."

"Well," she said, hardening her voice as her body went rigid again, "I hope it was worth it. I hope your mind is happy and healthy and whole, because that was not how you left me."

She turned her back on him and walked away, just like he'd done to her all those years ago.

And no, his mind was not happy and healthy and whole, and neither was his body.

You have Parkinson's disease.

The words, spoken by a doctor in Nashville, rang like a death knell in his ears. Sure, the diagnosis wasn't fatal, but it might as well be.

Because for someone like him, who needed freedom as much as he needed air, being trapped in a body that wouldn't cooperate was its own special kind of hell.

Chapter Nine

As Ian looked out over acres of gently rolling hills, he thought about how different Texas was from Montana. Obviously, he'd known that, had been through the state a time or two when he was in the military. He just hadn't paid attention back then.

But now he could feel it in the air and hear it in the chirps of birds and insects that weren't as common or that even existed up north. In this part of Texas, the green hills kept the horizon close. Back home, the land was flat as a sheet, dotted only by the odd plateau. You could see forever, all the way to the majestic mountains in the distance.

There was a certain appeal to Texas, but he had Montana in his blood, and he didn't think he'd survive long without real mountains within sight. The military had dragged him around for almost ten years, always stationing him in shitholes, and he'd missed the Rockies every single day. Back then, he'd hoped to show his son the mountains someday, but that wasn't going to happen now.

"Mr. Briggs? You sure you don't want to look at another property?"

Ian turned to the real estate agent, Grady, a middle-aged man whose plate-sized silver and turquoise belt buckle barely peeked out from beneath his beer belly. "I like this one."

"But it's no longer for sale." He dabbed at his sweaty brow with a blue handkerchief he plucked from his taupe suit jacket. People still used handkerchiefs? "Mr. Harlan just signed the papers."

"He signed yesterday. The ink isn't even dry yet, so he hasn't moved forward with his plans." Apparently, Griffin Harlan, some movie star, wanted the land for a vineyard and winery. He was calling it Hollywood & Vine, and the plan was to get star power behind the label. The wines would then be named after Hollywood legends and movies. Interesting concept.

"He won't sell," Grady insisted, "and even if he did, the price would be astronomical. Now, the adjacent property is for sale. It's half the size, but it's the closest property to Storm, and you said you didn't want anything too remote."

A truck came around the corner, but instead of passing by, it turned into the drive. Ian was surprised to see Zeke and Tucker Johnson get out, looking like they had serious bugs up their asses. It was a huge change from the last time he saw them, last night at the barbecue, with Tucker three sheets to the wind.

"Zeke. Tucker." Grady nodded at them both in greeting, and Ian did the same.

"What's going on here?" Zeke asked, skipping niceties.

Grady held up his hand in a placatory gesture, confusing the hell out of Ian. The Johnsons seemed ready to go to the mat over something, and hopefully Grady knew what it was because Ian was lost.

"Mr. Briggs is looking for some land for cattle," Grady said, "and since this property is still listed, he wanted to take a look."

"That's just a technicality. The property is sold." Zeke turned to Ian. "It couldn't be used for cattle anyway. It's been slated for a vineyard."

Zeke's defensiveness was curious, wasn't it? "What if Mr. Harlan decided to start a ranch on this property instead of a vineyard?"

"He can't do that," Grady said. "The purchase agreement specified what the land can and can't be used for."

That seemed odd. "Is that common practice in Texas? Who decides what the land can and can't be used for?"

"It's common here," Tucker said. "And we decided. We would have bought the land if the potential buyer wanted it for cattle."

Grady dabbed at his face again with the handkerchief. "Property owners around here have an agreement with the Johnsons. Anything over a certain acreage must first be offered to the Johnsons."

Suddenly, the reason Ian hadn't seen any other large ranches in the area made sense. "Ah. So you don't want the competition."

"Griffin Harlan's winery will bring a lot of money to Storm." Zeke's stance was aggressive, a clear message that he wouldn't tolerate a disruption in the way things were run around here. "It isn't that we can't handle a little competition," he said. "It's just that we need diversity in the area."

That was bullshit and Ian knew it. Zeke was protecting his own interests. "Is that why back in the day, you blocked the sale of the Weissman property when a buyer wanted it for cattle? But you didn't oppose the sale when a retail company needing warehouse space made an offer?"

Zeke's head snapped back in surprise. Tucker just looked confused. "How did you know about that?"

"Small town," Ian said with a shrug. Actually, he'd overheard someone laughing about it at the barbecue, one of those, "Remember when..." stories that was only funny if you'd been there. He wasn't sure if it was true or not, but he'd given it a shot. Looked like he hit the target.

Anger flashed in Zeke's expression. "It was nice that you came all the way down here to see Marcus, but as you can see, he's doing fine. So why don't you run on back to the wilds of Montana and let us handle our own business?"

Ian inhaled deeply, forcing himself to remain calm. Looking at property had been a bit of a lark, something he hadn't even been sure he wanted to do. But these jackasses had just solidified his wavering resolve. Marcus shouldn't be working for these pricks. He should have a ranch of his own.

And Ian was going to make sure he got it.

Chapter Ten

"Hey, Marcus, 'sup?"

Marcus grinned at Logan, who was washing glasses behind the bar at the pub his family owned. "I'm here to meet Ian." He glanced around and saw the man sitting in a booth near the back. He waved in acknowledgment, and Marcus waved back, giving him the universal "be there in a second" gesture. "Can I get a Harp?"

"Sure." Logan dried his hands and poured a glass of lager from the tap. "Is everything okay?"

"Yeah. Really good. Brittany's family is still trying to run me out of town, but that's old news."

Logan winced. "They did something new? Besides that article?"

"You didn't hear?" Marcus plopped a ten on the counter. "This morning the police came to our house because they got an anonymous call that women were heard screaming."

"Holy shit." Logan slid the glass of Harp to him and took the bill. "You got swatted?"

"Well, it was two overweight, old cops who couldn't break down a door if they teamed up *and* had a battering ram, but yeah. They were total dicks and my mom and sisters got stuck right in the middle of it. And then Brittany called to tell me she had to delete her Facebook account because she was getting so much harassment."

Logan's eyes shot wide as he handed Marcus change. "What the hell? Why are people harassing her?"

Anger soured his stomach. The shit she had to put up with made him sick with impotent anger. People were saying horrible things to her, threatening her, even, but he couldn't do a damned thing about it. Anonymous social media trolls sucked.

"Half of them think she's giving women a bad name for putting up with my worthless ass, and the other half are mad because they think she's hurting her father's campaign by dating a half-breed criminal."

"I'm sorry, man." Logan shook his head. "People are just damned stupid."

Marcus laughed. "And that, right there, is why I come to you for advice. You boil any problem down to its most basic form."

Logan shrugged. "I have a gift."

Shooting Logan a "you're hopeless" look, he grabbed his beer and joined Ian at the table.

"I'm glad you called," he told Ian. "Brittany is busy with school, and the Johnsons said they don't need me at the ranch today. They sent a lot of cattle to market recently, so I'm not working as many hours as I'd like."

Ian took a drink of his own beer. Judging by the color and Ian's preferences, Marcus guessed the beer was this month's special from a local craft brewery.

"That's what I called you here to talk about." At the gravity in Ian's voice, Marcus's gut dove straight to his feet, filling his boots.

"I don't like the sound of this..."

Ian smiled. "It's nothing bad, I promise." Still, he

seemed to need a moment to collect himself, and Marcus prepared for the worst. "You know how I feel about you, right? You're important to me. I couldn't love you more if you were my biological son."

Marcus swallowed. Hector hadn't, not once, said he loved Marcus. Not that Marcus would have believed it. But he definitely believed Ian, and his eyes stung with emotion.

"I feel the same way about you," Marcus said, trying to keep from choking up.

"I know." Ian leaned forward in his seat, propping his forearms on the table. "That's why I'm moving some of my business to Storm."

Marcus blinked, unsure he'd heard Ian right. "Business? You mean cattle?"

"Yep."

Marcus shook his head to clear it, but it didn't work. "At the risk of sounding like I've already drunk too much...I don't understand."

"You know how we've talked about buying pastureland near Missoula to start up an organic, grass-fed beef or bison operation?"

Expanding the business had been something Ian wanted to do for a while, and they'd often talked about establishing a specialized branch of Briggs Canyon Ranch, named after a canyon settled by Ian's ancestors in the late 1800s.

"Yeah." He paused as Logan dropped off a bowl of mixed nuts. "We talked about it again just before I left."

"Well, I could do it here instead. The Johnsons won't let anyone run a large operation in the area, but I did a lot of research, and Storm is in the perfect location for a small, grass-fed farm. And I want you to run it."

Marcus's mouth went dry. For the last couple of years Ian had made it clear that he wanted Marcus to take over for him someday, but honestly, Marcus had been afraid to believe it. Too much of his childhood had been spent waiting in vain for his dad to follow through on his promises.

So to have Ian actually do what he'd said...it left him stunned. But more than that, it was Ian's faith in Marcus that overwhelmed him.

"I don't...I don't know what to say." His voice was scratchy and raw, and so much for not choking up. "You want me to *run* it?"

"Not just run it, son. You'll be running it *with* me, not *for* me." Ian looked down at his glass, and when he lifted his gaze again, the unrestrained emotion in his eyes startled Marcus. "You'll be co-owner of the Storm business. That's if you want it. No pressure." He studied Marcus in that knowing way of his. "You don't look too thrilled. You don't have to do this—"

"No." Marcus's voice was little more than a frog's croak now. "No, I mean, I want it. I just don't know why you're offering it to me. You could find someone better. More experienced—"

"But no one I trust more than you."

Marcus's hand shook as emotion crashed over him. Ian didn't trust easily, so for him to say that about Marcus...it left him shaken. And when Marcus was shaken, he didn't handle it well. He never had. Old insecurities boiled up and walls long fallen started rebuilding. His self-defense mechanism had always been to push people away, and before he could stop himself from saying it, it came out.

"I don't need charity. I'm doing good here. I have a job and a girlfriend and—"

"Hey," Ian said, his voice level. Calm. Exactly what Marcus needed. "It's not charity and you know it. The only reason we didn't go ahead with this idea in Montana was because I didn't like the thought of moving you so far away. Not because I didn't trust you, but because I liked having you around. But now you're here and I still want my organic farm, so it only makes sense to set it up in Storm."

"Is that why you're here?" Marcus asked. "Why you came all the way to Texas?"

Ian reached down to the bench next to him and slapped a folder in the center of the table. "I came because I need your signature on some paperwork, and we need to have it notarized."

"What papers?"

"I'm giving you power of attorney over all Briggs Canyon Ranch's holdings, my estate, and pretty much everything else." Ian pushed the folder toward him. "I also made you the sole beneficiary of my estate, so I'm bringing you a copy of the will to hang on to."

Holy. Shit. Marcus's mouth dropped open. He forced it closed, but damn, he was going to hyperventilate. He really was.

"But...your family. You have a sister and a nephew in Utah."

Ian took a handful of nuts out of the bowl on the table. "I've never even met my nephew and I haven't spoken to my sister in decades. She sided with my wife in the divorce and didn't bother to even call when my son died." He washed the nuts down with beer. "She will never see a penny of my money."

Okay, he understood that. "But what if you meet someone...have kids—"

"Listen to me, Marcus." Ian slammed his glass down on the tabletop hard enough to slosh beer on his hand. "It doesn't matter. You will always have a place in my life—and in my will—equal to any natural born children I might have, and the Storm ranch will always be yours and yours alone."

The emotional overload was too much for Marcus. He felt as if his circuits were shorting out, leaving him unable to think and unsure what to feel. He had to get out of here. He needed air. Open space. If he was at the ranch, he'd be making a beeline for the stables to saddle a horse.

"I...excuse me."

He got out of there like the pub was on fire. The last time he'd done this, it had ended in a brawl with Logan. But this time he wasn't angry. He was happy. So why the hell was he freaking out?

He strode out into the parking lot and stood next to his car, marveling at how fortunate he'd been to knock on Ian's door when he'd been down on his luck. Ian had taken him in, even though it had been apparent that he hadn't needed more help.

Gradually, Marcus had learned Ian's story, how he and his wife had married young and divorced two years later, and thanks to his military deployments, she'd been awarded full custody of their toddler son. She'd remarried, and Ian had suspected that her new husband was a shitbag who abused her, but he couldn't prove anything, especially since he didn't live nearby and was always overseas.

Then, one day while stationed in some sandbox in the Middle East, he'd gotten a video message from his eight-year-old son. The kid had been crying, terrified of his stepfather. Ian had managed to get emergency leave, but when the plane touched down in Los Angeles, he'd been met by cops who told him that his son had been beaten to death.

The stepfather, who was the prime suspect, had disappeared, and Ian had hunted the bastard down and killed him. Ian spent a couple of years in jail on a light sentence, and when he got out on parole, he returned to the family ranch in Montana and tried to put himself back together.

Somehow, Ian had survived, and if he could go through all of that and come out of it without losing his mind, surely Marcus could handle his own, relatively minor, problems.

He heard Ian's boots clack on the pavement patio, but they stopped several feet away. Ian stood silently, the way Marcus knew he would, while he waited for Marcus to speak first.

They'd done this more times than Marcus could count. The first couple of times, Marcus had flipped out, screamed at Ian, getting in his face while the man just stood there like a damned statue. After failing to get a suitable, angry response, Marcus had stormed off. Which, of course, left him looking like a total dick when he had to face the guy again.

Frustrated by the awkwardness, Marcus had changed things up the third time. He'd taken a swing at Ian.

The punch never landed. In a blur of motion, Ian had taken Marcus to the ground, pinned him, and held him, face first, in the dirt until Marcus stopped struggling.

"You ready to stop being a complete jackass and start learning to deal with shit instead of fighting it?"

Marcus had growled...and earned some knee pressure against a nerve in his back he hadn't even known existed.

"Say again?" Ian had said calmly.

"Yes," Marcus had wheezed. "I'm ready."

The pressure had eased up, but Ian didn't let go. "Get this through your thick skull, son. You can get up, take another swing, and I'll take you down again. We can do it over and over, and I can promise you two things. One, you'll wear out before I do. And two, no matter what you do, I won't hit you. I have a feeling you've been through enough of that already. So we can go a few more rounds of bullshit and I'll win anyway, or we can skip all of that and you can get up and talk to me like a man. It's up to you." He'd kept Marcus pinned for another ten seconds to give him time to process, and then he'd backed off.

Something deep inside had told Marcus that this was a turning point. It was a life ring in a stormy sea, and if Marcus didn't take it, his future would be no different than his past.

So when Ian offered his hand, Marcus had taken it and let the other man pull him to his feet.

Which wasn't to say that things had been easy afterward. A broken truck window and fist-sized hole in the kitchen wall were proof of that.

Marcus shuddered, so ashamed of those days. "I don't deserve this, Ian. I was such an asshole to you. I pushed you away over and over. I took a swing at you. I broke your truck window, and your wall, and your—"

"All true," Ian said calmly. "You were a disaster."

"Then why?" Marcus shook his head, unable to fathom that anyone could be so patient. So decent. "Why did you keep trying? And don't tell me I reminded you of your son. There's no way he was like me."

"He liked cows."

Marcus blinked. "What?"

Ian let out a long, deep breath. "You want to know why I didn't give up on you? Because believe me, I gave it a thought once or twice. But it was the way you were when you were alone with the cattle or the horses that made me see the real you. See, no matter how angry you were, you never lost patience with the animals. If anything, they calmed you down. Think about when and where we had our best talks."

"Sitting on the corral fence."

"Yeah." Ian's voice, still behind Marcus, was a little closer now. "Whenever you were upset, no matter what time of day or night or no matter what the weather, you always went out and sat on the fence and looked at the mountains."

"The cows liked it when I scratched their backs with my boots."

"That's how I knew I was right about you. You understood that doing something nice made you feel good. A lot of men hurt things to make themselves feel better. Men like Hector. And the bastard who killed my boy." His hand came down on Marcus's shoulder. "When I say you reminded me of my son, it's because I saw the good in you."

"You saw the bad in me, too. It's still there, Ian. It's not like it's a constant struggle to keep it at bay or anything, but sometimes when I get really mad..." He blew out a breath and stared at the hood of his car.

"That's normal, kid. Jesus, who doesn't want to throw a punch now and then? And there are times when you have to. Just don't beat yourself up over it."

"Beat *myself* up?" He turned to Ian, but he couldn't look him in the face. "I nearly beat up my sister's boyfriend a while ago. And every time I see Senator Rush I want to pound him into the dirt for how he treated Dakota. And for being a slime in general."

"You're not giving yourself credit for not doing those things. It takes more strength to rein yourself in than it does to give in to your anger."

Marcus laughed and finally looked up at his mentor. "Look at you, all Obi-Wan."

"I've just learned a lot of hard lessons." Ian hooked his thumbs in his jeans pockets. "What's really going on with you, Marcus? Something's been eating at you. Is it me?"

"No," Marcus said, taken aback. He didn't think he could ever be angry with Ian again. "Hell, no. It's just...everything's going so good. Like a fairy tale. This is too good to be true, you know? But then there's my dad. And Brittany."

"What about them? Are you and Brittany having trouble?"

He shook his head. "Not really. I mean, it's not *us*. It's her family. They're trying to tear us apart. I've been telling people I'm not worried about it, but the truth is that I'm afraid that one day they'll succeed. And the thing with my dad..." He swallowed. "I'm scared, Ian. Shit, I'm scared."

Marcus felt like a fool admitting that. He hadn't even admitted it to Logan. Or Brittany, to whom he could tell almost anything. But Ian didn't even bat an eye, not that Marcus expected anything else.

"You're stronger and more disciplined than he is," Ian said. "You know how to defend yourself. You don't need to be afraid of him anymore. He can't hurt you."

Marcus snorted. "I'm not afraid *of* him. And that's what scares me." He looked Ian in the eye, knowing this was the one person in the world who wouldn't judge him. "I'm afraid he'll come back, and I'm afraid of what I'll do if he does."

Chapter Eleven

Ian gripped the steering wheel hard as he drove away from Murphy's, anger steaming in his veins. It had killed him to watch Marcus struggle to accept love.

Oh, he'd seen those reactions before, back when Marcus was still half-feral, like an abused dog dumped in the woods. He'd been wary, reactive, and self-destructive. When faced with kindness, he retreated or lashed out. It had taken a long time, but eventually he'd learned that Ian's kindness wasn't a trick to lure him in and then hurt him.

But this was different. Marcus had known he was important to Ian, but he'd clearly not known *how* important. Or maybe he hadn't believed it. It wasn't as if he'd had a good, or even marginal, role model when it came to men.

Hector Alvarez was damned lucky he wasn't in town right now, because Ian didn't know if he was strong enough to resist the impulse to hunt him down.

And he really didn't need to go to jail again for the same crime.

But damn that son of a bitch to hell. Marcus didn't seem to know where Hector had gone, and Ian wasn't ashamed to admit he hoped the guy was feeding vultures in a ravine somewhere.

He turned left and saw the realtor's office up ahead. Now he needed more than land for his new cattle venture. He also needed to find an apartment to rent. Sure, he could handle some of the new operation from Montana, but it made more sense to do it from here. And Marcus needed him.

And now that he was planning on a lengthier stay than he'd first anticipated, he could make some other plans.

Like paying a visit to Marisol Moreno.

* * * *

Hector Alvarez sat beneath the shade of a sun-bleached patio umbrella at the roadside burger joint where he'd stopped for lunch. He was two hours from Storm, and the closer he got, the more his anger consumed him.

Thanks to his bitch of a wife, he'd not only been run out of his own damn town, he'd wound up pissing off another asshole sheriff and spent six weeks in a goddamned jailhouse. Son of a bitch had confiscated his guns and trumped up an illegal weapons charge.

He took a bite of his barbecue bacon burger, trying to calm down and then made the mistake of looking down at the picture on his phone again. Bile filled his mouth at the sight of his wife—his fucking *wife*—with the very man who had run Hector out of Storm.

The average person wouldn't see anything but two friends chatting inside Murphy's Pub. Nothing to see here, folks.

But Hector knew better. The look Joanne was giving Dillon Murphy was one he hadn't seen in years. The one that said she wanted to go down on her knees and put those plump lips where all women should keep them.

Fucking bitch. She hadn't wanted to do that to Hector since their damned honeymoon. Oh, she did it, but only under protest. But she couldn't protest with her mouth full, could she?

Anger pumped through his veins like acid as he slid his thumb over the phone's sauce-smeared surface to bring up the second of two pictures Marylee Rush had texted to him. This one was of Marcus. He was at some sort of gathering, standing next to a dark-haired man whose hand rested on Marcus's shoulder.

Who the hell was the guy?

Hector reached for a greasy French fry and went to switch his phone to call mode, but his thumb slipped and flipped to another photo he'd gotten yesterday. This one had come from an anonymous source, was grainy and blurry, but just clear enough to recognize one of the two people in it.

Instantly, his hunger turned to nausea, and he dropped the fry. The picture was too disgusting to contemplate.

With a growl, he dialed the phone and waited for Dakota to answer. When she did, hearing her voice made him grin despite the fact that he was disappointed in her. "Hey, sweetheart."

"Daddy?" she gasped. "Oh, my God, is it really you?"

"Yeah." He kept an eye on the state trooper who had just pulled into the parking lot. Considering a crazy-ass sheriff had run him out of Storm, Hector wasn't feeling too cozy with law enforcement types. Not that he ever did. "It's me."

"Where are you? Are you okay? Are you coming home?"

"Slow down, Dakota." The cop gave him a passing glance as he got out of his cruiser and headed toward the food shack. "I'll answer your questions, but first, tell me how you've been."

There was a second of silence, and he wondered if she was planning on lying to him. "Oh, Daddy, it's been so hard without you. I hate this town and I hate everyone in it. And it got so much worse after you left." She inhaled. "Why *did* you leave?"

Because the sheriff is a self-righteous prick. But he'll get what's coming to him.

"It's a long story," he said, "but don't worry. You'll know soon enough."

"Does that mean you're coming home?"

Not yet. But soon. He was going to stay with a friend near Storm, where he'd watch and wait until the perfect time to drop in on his family.

"Well, that depends," he said. "How's your mother doing?"

"Fine, I guess. She's working for Tate Johnson."

He tasted bile. Tate was wealthy, handsome, and a real prick. Joanne better not be whoring for him. "What about your sister?"

"Mallory's Mallory. She's mad because she's getting a B-plus in math."

That made him crack a smile. Dakota had always been his favorite, especially since Marcus turned out to be such a disappointment, but Mallory was the most intelligent of his spawn. Hell, she was the smartest person in the whole family. "And Marcus?"

She huffed. "Why are you asking all of this? Why aren't you coming home?"

"Dakota, honey," he said through clenched teeth, his patience wearing thin, "tell me about your brother."

She huffed again. "He's fine. He's working for the Johnsons, and he's all happy because Ian's here."

"Ian?" He frowned. The name sounded familiar. "Who the hell is Ian?"

"He's the guy Marcus worked for in Montana. He's buying Marcus a ranch or something."

Hector jerked like someone had jabbed him with a cattle prod, and the picture Marylee had sent popped into his mind. He'd bet his left nut that the guy in the photo was Ian. And wait, he was buying Marcus a ranch? What the hell for?

Marcus couldn't run a lawnmower without fucking up. How was he supposed to run a damned ranch?

"This Ian guy had better not be sniffing around your mother," he growled. "Or you."

"Gross." She paused to take a drink of something. "He's too old for me."

"But Senator Rush wasn't?"

Silenced settled over the airwaves. "Daddy," she whispered. "I can explain."

Good luck explaining the picture someone sent of you going down on the senator. Oh, the man in the picture wasn't clear, and his head had been cut off so there would never be any solid proof, but Hector had known exactly whose expensive slacks had been bunched around Dakota's not-so-innocent face.

Hector kept his tone civil. There would be plenty of time to right all the wrongs that had been done while he'd been away.

"And you will explain," he said calmly. "But not now. Now...now I want you to promise you won't tell anyone you've heard from me. I'll be home soon, baby girl, and I want it to be a surprise."

There would be a lot of surprises. He'd been gone for a while, but his time spent in Del Rio hadn't been a total waste. He'd gotten in with a rough crowd, people who had sworn to help him hide bodies if he needed them to.

And he might. There were a whole lot of people who had better watch their backs, and he didn't give a shit if they were sheriffs, senators, Montana ranchers...or his own bastard son.

* * * *

The story continues with Episode 3, Brave the Storm by Lisa Mondello.

About Larissa Ione

Air Force veteran Larissa Ione traded in a career as a meteorologist to pursue her passion of writing. She has since published dozens of books, hit several bestseller lists, including the New York Times and USA Today, and has been nominated for a RITA award. She now spends her days in pajamas with her computer, strong coffee, and fictional worlds. She believes in celebrating everything, and would never be caught without a bottle of Champagne chilling in the fridge...just in case. After a dozen moves all over the country with her now-retired U.S. Coast Guard spouse, she is now settled in Wisconsin with her husband, her teenage son, a rescue cat named Vegas, and her very own hellhound, a King Shepherd named Hexe.

For more information about Larissa, visit www.larissaione.com.

Sign up for the Rising Storm/1001 Dark Nights Newsletter
and be entered to win an exclusive lightning bolt necklace
specially designed for Rising Storm by
Janet Cadsawan of Cadsawan.com.

Go to www.RisingStormBooks.com to subscribe.

As a bonus, all subscribers will receive a free
Rising Storm story
Storm Season: Ginny & Jacob – the Prequel
by Dee Davis

Rising Storm

Storm, Texas.

Where passion runs hot, desire runs deep, and secrets have the power to destroy…

Nestled among rolling hills and painted with vibrant wildflowers, the bucolic town of Storm, Texas, seems like nothing short of perfection.

But there are secrets beneath the facade. Dark secrets. Powerful secrets. The kind that can destroy lives and tear families apart. The kind that can cut through a town like a tempest, leaving jealousy and destruction in its wake, along with shattered hopes and broken dreams. All it takes is one little thing to shatter that polish.

Rising Storm is a series conceived by Julie Kenner and Dee Davis to read like an on-going drama. Set in a small Texas town, *Rising Storm* is full of scandal, deceit, romance, passion, and secrets. Lots of secrets.

Look for other Rising Storm Season 2 titles, now available! (And if you missed Season 1 and the midseason episodes, you can find those titles here!)

Rising Storm, Season Two

Against the Wind by Rebecca Zanetti
As Tate Johnson works to find a balance between his

ambitions for political office and the fallout of his brother's betrayal, Zeke is confronted with his brother Chase's return home. And while Bryce and Tara Daniels try to hold onto their marriage, Kristin continues to entice Travis into breaking his vows...

Storm Warning by Larissa Ione
As Joanne Alvarez settles into life without Hector, her children still struggle with the fallout. Marcus confronts the differences between him and Brittany, while Dakota tries to find a new equilibrium. Meanwhile, the Johnson's grapple with war between two sets of brothers, and Ian Briggs rides into town...

Brave the Storm by Lisa Mondello
As Senator Rush's poll numbers free fall, Marylee tries to drive a wedge between Brittany and Marcus. Across town, Anna Mae and Chase dance toward reconciliation. Ginny longs for Logan, while he fights against Sebastian's maneuvering. And Hector, newly freed from prison, heads back to Storm...

Lightning Strikes by Lexi Blake
As Ian Briggs begins to fall for Marisol, Joanne and Dillon also grow closer. Joanne's new confidence spreads to Dakota but Hector's return upends everything. A public confrontation between Marcus and Hector endangers his relationship with Brittany, and Dakota reverts to form. Meanwhile, the Senator threatens Ginny and the baby...

Fire and Rain by R.K. Lilley
As Celeste Salt continues to unravel in the wake of Jacob's death, Travis grows closer with Kristin. Lacey realizes the error of her ways but is afraid it's too late for reconciliation with her friends. Marcus and Brittany struggle

with the continued fallout of Hector's return, while Chase and Anna Mae face some hard truths about their past...

Quiet Storm by Julie Kenner

As Mallory Alvarez and Luis Moreno grow closer, Lacey longs for forgiveness. Brittany and Marcus have a true meeting of hearts. Meanwhile, Jeffry grapples with his father's failures and finds solace in unexpected arms. When things take a dangerous turn, Jeffry's mother and sister, as well as his friends, unite behind him as the Senator threatens his son...

Blinding Rain by Elisabeth Naughton

As Tate Johnson struggles to deal with his brother's relationship with Hannah, hope asserts itself in an unexpected way. With the return of Delia Burke, Logan's old flame, Brittany and Marcus see an opportunity to help their friend. But when the evening takes an unexpected turn, Brittany finds herself doing the last thing she expected—coming face to face with Ginny...

Blue Skies by Dee Davis

As Celeste Salt struggles to pull herself and her family together, Dillon is called to the scene of a domestic dispute where Dakota is forced to face the truth about her father. While the Johnson's celebrate a big announcement, Ginny is rushed to the hospital where her baby's father is finally revealed...

Rising Storm, Midseason

After the Storm by Lexi Blake

In the wake of Dakota's revelations, the whole town is reeling. Ginny Moreno has lost everything. Logan Murphy is devastated by her lies. Brittany Rush sees her family in a horrifying new light. And nothing will ever be the same...

Distant Thunder by Larissa Ione
As Sebastian and Marylee plot to cover up Sebastian's sexual escapade, Ginny and Dakota continue to reel from the fallout of Dakota's announcement. But it is the Rush family that's left to pick up the pieces as Payton, Brittany and Jeffry each cope with Sebastian's betrayal in their own way...

Rising Storm, Season One

Tempest Rising by Julie Kenner
Ginny Moreno didn't mean to do it, but when she came home to Storm, she brought the tempest with her. And now everyone will be caught in its fury...

White Lightning by Lexi Blake
As the citizens of Storm, Texas, sway in the wake of the death of one of their own, Daddy's girl Dakota Alvarez also reels from an unexpected family crisis ... and finds consolation in a most unexpected place.

Crosswinds by Elisabeth Naughton
Lacey Salt's world shattered with the death of her brother, and now the usually sweet-tempered girl is determined to take back some control—even if that means sabotaging her best friend, Mallory, and Mallory's new boyfriend, Luis.

Dance in the Wind by Jennifer Probst
During his time in Afghanistan, Logan Murphy has endured the unthinkable, but reentering civilian life in Storm is harder than he imagined. But when he is reacquainted with Ginny Moreno, a woman who has survived terrors of her

own, he feels the first stirrings of hope.

Calm Before the Storm by Larissa Ione

Marcus Alvarez fled Storm when his father's drinking drove him over the edge. With his mother and sisters in crisis, Marcus is forced to return to the town he thought he'd left behind. But it is his attraction to a very grown up Brittany Rush that just might be enough to guarantee that he stays.

Take the Storm by Rebecca Zanetti

Marisol Moreno has spent her youth taking care of her younger siblings. Now, with her sister, Ginny, in crisis, and her brother in the throes of his first real relationship, she doesn't have time for anything else. Especially not the overtures of the incredibly compelling Patrick Murphy.

Weather the Storm by Lisa Mondello

Bryce Douglas faces a crisis of faith when his idyllic view of his family is challenged with his son's diagnosis of autism. Instead of accepting his wife and her tight-knit family's comfort, he pushes them away, fears from his past threatening to undo the happiness he's found in his present.

Thunder Rolls by Dee Davis
In the season finale …

As Hannah Grossman grapples with the very real possibility that she is dating one Johnson brother while secretly in love with another, the entire town prepares for Founders Day. The building tempest threatens not just Hannah's relationship with Tucker and Tate, but everyone in Storm as dire revelations threaten to tear the town apart.

Brave the Storm
Rising Storm, Season 2, Episode 3
By Lisa Mondello
Now Available

Secrets, Sex and Scandals ...

Welcome to Storm, Texas, where passion runs hot, desire runs deep, and secrets have the power to destroy... Get ready. The storm is coming.

As Senator Rush's poll numbers free fall, Marylee tries to drive a wedge between Brittany and Marcus. Across town, Anna Mae and Chase dance toward reconciliation. Ginny longs for Logan, while he fights against Sebastian's maneuvering. And Hector, newly freed from prison, heads back to Storm...

* * * *

"Are you going to hang around this house brooding all day again?" Rita Mae asked, dropping the last of the morning dishes into the dishwasher.

Most of the guests they'd had overnight had either checked out or gone about their business of the day. The house was quiet and Anna Mae was ready to dive into a long list of tasks she'd written out on a notepad last night before bed.

"What are you talking about?" Anna Mae asked as she reviewed her list. She knew. She always knew. Anna Mae just wasn't in the mood for another one of Rita Mae's lectures.

Mary Louise came into the kitchen dressed more formally for the day than she normally did. "I'm not sure when I'll be home tonight," she said.

Rita Mae tilted a curious eyebrow. "Oh, no? Why not?"

"Why is she not sure or why won't she be home?" Anna Mae asked.

"Both."

"Leave the girl alone. She's young. She's probably got herself a hot date." Anna Mae winked at her niece.

Mary Louise grabbed a glass from the cabinet and then went to the refrigerator and poured a glass of orange juice before answering. "I could say the same of you."

"Me?" Anna Mae laughed. "Don't be ridiculous. I'm too old for *hot* dates."

"Don't say that. Please don't say that," Mary Louise said. "I can't bear the thought that romance dies and love goes stale as we get older. I haven't even had a real turn at it."

"Oh, so it *is* a hot date," Rita Mae said. "I saw you talking with Tate Johnson at the barbeque yesterday. Are you seeing him?"

"It's a meeting. That's all. Tate and Hannah broke up and we're...we're just friends."

"But you'd like it to be more?" Rita Mae asked.

Mary Louise shrugged as a blush crept up her cheeks. "Besides, now that Chase Johnson is back in town, why shouldn't you have a hot date, Anna Mae?"

Anna Mae dropped the pencil she'd been using to add notes to her list as shock took hold.

"Why would you say something like that?" she said, feigning ignorance.

"Oh, come on. It may have been a long time ago but Dad told me you and Chase were once an item. I even saw an old picture of the two of you hugging."

"You did?" Rita Mae asked.

"Yeah. Dad and Chase were both playing at some club. It didn't look like much more than a rinky-dink honkytonk. That's what my mother used to call them. Of course, Mom had a thing for hanging out with Dad at those honkytonks. Do you remember, Anna Mae?"

There were too many places like that to remember which one Mary Louise could be talking about. Too many late nights with too much drink and too many years that made it all fuzzy now.

And she could lie to herself about how much she remembered, but Anna Mae had made a career of silently cataloguing all those moments with Chase Johnson over the years. Perhaps that's why her anger had grown exponentially over the years after she'd told him to leave. She could have stopped him. And he would have stayed. She was sure of that. They'd loved each other so very much.

But Anna Mae couldn't bear the thought of the bitterness that would have grown inside of him for giving up his dream of playing music. Her brother had followed the same path, although he had tried for many years to make a go at family on the road.

Would it have been different if Anna Mae had followed Chase to Nashville? It was a question that she'd rolled over in her mind for many years on many nights while missing the feel of Chase's arms around her.

1001 Dark Nights

Welcome to 1001 Dark Nights… a collection of novellas that are breathtakingly sexy and magically romantic. Some are paranormal, some are erotic. Each and every one is compelling and page turning.

Inspired by the exotic tales of The Arabian Nights, 1001 Dark Nights features *New York Times* and *USA Today* bestselling authors.

In the original, Scheherazade desperately attempts to entertain her husband, the King of Persia, with nightly stories so that he will postpone her execution.

In our version, month after month, each of our fabulous authors puts a unique spin on the premise and creates a tale that a new Scheherazade tells long into the dark, dark night.

For more information about 1001 Dark Nights, visit www.1001DarkNights.com.

On behalf of Rising Storm,

Liz Berry, M.J. Rose, Julie Kenner & Dee Davis would like
to thank ~

Steve Berry
Doug Scofield
Melissa Rheinlander
Kim Guidroz
Jillian Stein
InkSlinger PR
Asha Hossain
Chris Graham
Pamela Jamison
Fedora Chen
Jessica Johns
Dylan Stockton
Richard Blake
The Dinner Party Show
and Simon Lipskar